Praise for *Si...*

"*Silver Alert* is Lee Smith at the top of her game, and that is a high bar indeed. It's brilliantly paced with some of the most energetic prose I've ever had the pleasure of reading. The characters of Herb Atlas and Dee Dee are a pair for the ages, who you will long remember after the fall of the last page."
—David Baldacci, author of *Dream Town*

"Bursting with life and laughter and love, an absolute delight. Smith's . . . story is compelling and her theme is uplifting. *Silver Alert* will make you laugh hard and feel hope . . . And that is a huge gift."
—*Minneapolis Star Tribune*

"*Silver Alert* is classic Lee Smith: laugh-out-loud funny and deeply moving, full of endearing, complex characters who become real people to the reader. This story of an elderly man who takes 'one last joyride' in his Porsche—with a young, mysterious manicurist aboard—is a lovely, raucous look at life in Key West, growing old, and unlikely friendships."
—Silas House, author of *Lark Ascending*

"There are many ways to read Lee Smith's excellent new novel *Silver Alert*, but I view it as the toll old age has taken on her characters, with all its indignities and absurdities, as well as a wry view of America itself. Staged in iconic Key West, the improviser's paradise, it's an implied prayer for our expressing kindness in gestures large and small."
—Ann Beattie, author of *The Accomplished Guest*

"High-velocity prose filled with humor and sweet compassion . . . Smith tackles very difficult material . . . with remarkable touch . . . Strikingly upbeat." —TopTenBooks

"This hilarious, timely, and emotional novel will reframe the way you think about the golden years. Herb and Renee's friendship leads to a high-octane twist that will leave you breathless. *Silver Alert* is a shimmering arrow that aims straight for the heart." —Adriana Trigiani, author of *The Good Left Undone*

Silver Alert

ALSO BY LEE SMITH

Silver Alert

a novel by

LEE SMITH

ALGONQUIN BOOKS
OF CHAPEL HILL
2024

Published by
ALGONQUIN BOOKS OF CHAPEL HILL
Post Office Box 2225
Chapel Hill, North Carolina 27515-2225

an imprint of WORKMAN PUBLISHING, a division of
HACHETTE BOOK GROUP, INC.
1290 Avenue of the Americas
New York, New York 10104

Printed in the United States of America
Design by Steve Godwin

Library of Congress Cataloging-in-Publication Data

Names: Smith, Lee, [date]– author.
Title: Silver alert / a novel by Lee Smith.
Description: First edition. | Chapel Hill, North Carolina :
Algonquin Books of Chapel Hill, 2023. |
Summary: "The story of an elderly man who, rather than give up his
independence, heads off on a joyride with a new young friend"
— Provided by publisher.
Identifiers: LCCN 2022049236 | ISBN 9781643752419 (hardcover) |
ISBN 9781643753737 (ebook)
Subjects: LCGFT: Novels.
Classification: LCC PS3569.M5376 S55 2023 |
DDC 813/.54—dc23/eng/20221019
LC record available at https://lccn.loc.gov/2022049236

ISBN 978-1-64375-580-9 (paperback)

10 9 8 7 6 5 4 3 2 1

First Paperback Edition

~ For Hal, again and always ~

CONTENTS

Silver Alert

House of Cards

~~~~~~

The doorbell rings promptly at 10 a.m. (exactly when Pat said), sending its jazzy little Hawaiian tune throughout the stately rooms of their big pink tropical house—hell, mansion is more like it—in Key West: 108 Washington Street, a primo address only one block from the classy Casa Marina Hotel and also Louie's Backyard restaurant, also classy, also pink. Too much pink in this goddamn town for a man, a real man anyway, a man like Herb used to be, yeah right, ha. Shit. Their house would go for a coupla mil right now. The song sounds again through the scented air of the solarium, big flowers blooming everyplace in here, Susan used to love them so, bless her soul and damn it all to hell.

"We are going to a hukilau . . ." Herbert Atlas sings along as he pads across the marble floor in his lime-green crocs toward the carved mahogany front door, his red-and-black plaid pajama pants held up by his considerable gut. The blue-flowered Hawaiian shirt is open three buttons down, exposing curly white chest hair. But shit. He's gotta pee again already, he's only been up since 8:30 and he's peed, what? Five or six times. Old age is all about urine, who knew? Who woulda thunk it?, as his first wife Roxana used to say, back in the day, that sainted woman, bless her soul, too.

Herb crosses the black-and-white vestibule to throw the deadbolt and turn the large brass knob.

The girl stands before him in a patch of sunlight that falls through thick palm fronds to surround her like a spotlight. She's smiling already. She looks like a kid, with those wide brown eyes beneath the blond bangs, her high, shiny pony-tail swinging as she steps forward in her white, white tennis shoes. They look brand new. She wears jeans and some kind of a pink tunic, professional looking.

"Atlas residence? Pedicure?" Her voice is low, nice.

"Yeah, that's right. I'm the husband, Herbert Atlas, call me Herb."

"But I was contacted by a Miss Pat DeVine . . ." The girl twitches her nose as she pulls a little notebook out of her big sparkly purse and looks at it.

"Yeah, yeah, that's right, that's my wife's daughter's part-ner, if you can follow that, but what the hell, this is Key West, isn't it? You got all kinda situations down here, am I right?"

The girl grins at him, one snaggletooth, which is adorable.

"So this pedicure is for my wife Susan, she's the one get-ting this pedicure, if you can get her to sit still long enough to get it. She's got some kind of toe problem going on, Jesus, who knows? I can't take her back to the salon where she used to go, over on Simonton, they said she caused a disturbance over there, this classy lady. Well, you'll see. Oh, you'll see. So now her daughter, that's Maribeth, she's the hippie one, and Maribeth's partner, that's Pat that called you, she's the bossy one, they've come down here for a couple months to see how Susan's doing, to help me take care of her, that's a crock. I never asked them, you understand. I don't need them, this is a classy operation. But this Pat, you can't tell her no, you can't tell her nothing."

The girl smiles steadily at Herb, her head cocked like a bird, listening. She acts like she's got all the time in the world.

"Sorry." Herb hitches up his pajama pants. "Well, you can give it a try." Then he remembers to ask: "Your name, honey?"

"Renee Martin." She holds out her pretty manicured hand. "Pleased to meet you."

Herb is beyond charmed. "Likewise." He gives her hand a quick squeeze. "Come on then. What the hell." He steps back and holds the door open, only then noticing the big, boxy bag she lifts up to carry along with the sparkly purse, and something else that looks like a tool kit. "Hey, can I help you with some of that?" he asks, too late.

"Oh no," Renee says, and clearly means it, almost prancing through the door.

Youth, he's thinking. Ah, youth.

She follows him through the solarium and down the hall to the left, through the gazebo garden and into the guest wing, which is now devoted to Susan, to Susan's care, goddamnit, and Herb doesn't care what anybody else thinks about it, he thinks he's doing a goddamn good job of it, and it's going fine. It's all going fine.

Under the circumstances.

He rings the bell twice, his regular signal. This time it's Cheri or Shari or maybe Kari, whatever her name is, from the islands, speaks with a lilt. He's got them coming around the clock.

She opens the door. "Mister Atlas, where you been? I tried to call you on the telephone, two time. You no answer your phone." Her musical voice has gone up an octave.

Damn it, Herb's thinking. "What's wrong, honey?" he says. He's got to pee something awful.

Cheri or Kari opens the door further. "Okay. You come in then, you see what she do here, you looka here at this mess. And you looka here at my arm. You see what she do, she cut me, Mister Atlas, she break the plate and then she won't give it to me and then I pull it away and it cut me right here—" A bloody dish towel is tied around her thin dark arm. "I cannot do this no more. I call Rita already."

Damn it to Hell. Rita runs the Island Home Health Agency. "Well, I'm real sorry, honey, but you'd better let me in."

Cheri/Kari opens the door and Herb steps in, surprised that Renee's right behind him, like his little shadow, he figured she'd get the hell out of Dodge while the getting was good.

So it's gone up to another level now. Susan, his once very charming third wife Susan, is having a really bad day, maybe her worst so far. You can always tell it's gonna be bad when she won't sit down but stands up drumming her hands like this on the countertop, like the goddamn Little Drummer Boy.

"Susan," he says. "Oh honey."

"Rat-a-tat-tat, rat-a-tat-tat," she chants, glaring at them, drumming. The small kitchen area is strewn with dishes and silverware, a barstool turned over, milk spilled on the floor.

"Oh baby." Herb steps forward to touch her but she pulls away, still drumming on the countertop. "Rat-a-tat, rat-a tat," she chants. Then "I hate you," she hisses at him. She sticks out her tongue. Something new. Susan's whole face is different now, like it's, what? What's the word? Warped or something. It's impossible to believe what a beautiful woman she was, and not that long ago, either. Herb massages her shoulder, chilled to the bone when she turns to stare at him with nothing, absolutely nothing in those blue eyes that look too big for her thin face now. "You go away," she says. "I hate you."

"That's what she been saying all morning. She hate everybody today." Cheri/Kari starts to clean things up, obviously relieved that he's there.

"She doesn't really hate anybody," Herb says, for Renee's benefit, and the girl answers unexpectedly, "I know," while Susan keeps on drumming on the countertop wearing her beautiful flowered silk robe from better days. She looks terrible of course, Herb realizes even more now with the girl here, Susan is really scary-looking with her hair standing up like that, all the blond growing out and the rest of it gray, like iron or something, and since he can't get her to the beauty salon, the home health girls have also been doing some powder thing to her hair and it looks like hell, he sees that now.

"Sorry, back in a minute!" Herb makes a break for the bathroom, which is a wreck, too, shit on the seat. Tough morning. Well the girls have got those Depends to deal with, he can't blame Cheri/Kari one bit, or any of them.

"Now you wait just a damn minute here, please," Herb starts, not knowing what he can possibly say under these shitty circumstances—he almost has to grin at that—but Cheri/Kari's gone, she's out the door, he hears her lilting voice raised as she starts going on and on to somebody who must be right there in the gazebo, must be Pat, that calm, level voice, which for once Herb is glad to hear. Okay, things are getting out of hand here. He goes to the door to join them, then realizes he can't leave the guest house, he can't leave Susan alone with this girl who doesn't even know her.

TURNING BACK, HERB is surprised to find Susan silent for once. She's sitting calmly in the big puffy rattan chair by the bay window, only her fingers moving over its creamy cushioned arms, staring fixedly at Renee who moves around the chair singing something—singing? What is she singing, it sounds familiar but who knows what they sing anymore, young people? Renee leans over to open up that toolbox thing on the floor, which turns out to be like a little showcase displaying all the tools of her trade. Lotsa little different colored bottles, some shiny, pointy silver things that look dangerous to Herb, he starts to say something but does not because Susan sits so still now, watching Renee, who keeps singing while she opens up the other bag and gets out this fancy fake marble tub thing, which she fills up at the kitchen sink and then places at Susan's feet, plugging a cord into the outlet beside the big chair. What the hell? Herb thinks, then he realizes: hot. She's gotta heat it up for the pedicure. Who knew so much would be involved here?

Herb sits down in the breakfast nook to watch. Now Renee kneels right down on the soft blue carpet in front of Susan to take off her golden slippers—from an earlier, better time, Jesus!—and picks up her bony feet one by one to place them in the water. Renee throws some kind of salts or powder stuff or something in the water, too, which fizzes up and gets bubbly now. "Somewhere over the rainbow . . ." Renee keeps on singing and Susan sits perfectly still, it's like she's hypnotized. Herb can't believe he's seeing this.

Renee leans forward and slips from singing into speaking in a soft, musical voice that is much like a song itself. "Oh my goodness now, you just relax, Miss Susan, you're so tired aren't you, sweetie? I know how tired you are, doesn't this feel good now" as she massages Susan's feet one by one for a long time, examining each toe carefully, nodding before she places them back into the bubbly water, which shines iridescent as the sun from the bay window creeps across the blue carpet. Susan nods and relaxes, you can see her shoulders slump as the girl massages her long, skinny legs one by one, slowly, slowly, singing again but softly now. This goes on for a long time.

Herb relaxes, too, leaning back in the breakfast nook. Susan. Goddamn. Susan who looked like a goddamn fashion model the first time he ever saw her, this was what? Only twelve years ago, at a big party for the opening of a show in her art gallery, her own classy art gallery in that building of his in Palm Beach. Herb only attended that party because Marco made him, he almost didn't go, he wanted to get a steak at Shula's instead—shit, what if he hadn't gone? Because then he never would have met Susan Summerville with those long, long legs that go on forever, a woman like a long drink of water on a hot day. Herb doesn't mind a tall woman himself, a woman taller than he is, what the hell. Or a big woman, or a heavy woman. Herb just likes women, all kinds of women. But this Susan Summerville, she was something else, something new for Herb, an educated woman, an artistic woman, a cultured woman. Turned out she'd opened the gallery mostly to sell her own husband's paintings since he'd crashed his plane in some Louisiana swamp. This husband had been a wild man from all accounts, Cajun or something, a good painter everybody said, though Herb couldn't see it, these paintings didn't look like whatever the guy was supposed to be painting, they were all wavy and weird. But what the hell. Herb bought two big ones at the opening, $4500 and $6800, and took Susan Summerville out to Shula's with him afterward, where she did not order the steak. She ordered some kind of raw fish thing instead, and champagne. She thought he was funny, she kept laughing at him. She had this way of throwing her long hair back and winking at you. So the next day he showed up at her gallery at noon to take her out to lunch, but she just laughed at him some more. "I can't do that!" she said. "I'm the only one here, I'm running this gallery on a shoestring, that's the whole idea." Turns out she was raising money to send her kids to college. She said she couldn't go out to dinner that night either, she had a commitment.

"Well, whaddya want to do, then, honey?" Herb had asked, sitting down in a weird arty chair. "Look, this is a courtship. This is my courtship of you. And I'm old, so I don't wanna waste any time here. You better take advantage of me. So whaddya want to do? Look, I'm ready for some culture, just try me. Expand my damn horizons."

The upshot of it was, they went to Paris. Then Barcelona. Then the Serengeti. They saw paintings and cathedrals and lions. He bought her a Tanzanite ring at Harry Winston in New York, they stayed in a suite at the Four Seasons.

His daughters had hit the roof.

"Daddy, what do you think you're doing?" Ashley said at the time. "It's not fair to her, you're too old. She'll just have to take care of you. That's not fair, is it?"

And his daughter Marcie said, "She just wants your money."

"Listen," he'd said. "Susan Summerville has got her own money"—which was not quite true—"and she is a damn sweet lady. A Southern lady." Which was true, goddamnit, she'd made her damn debut in New Orleans and she had the best manners in the world, and the best taste.

Turned out his girls loved her the minute they met her, of course, and his son, Brian, too. And his previous wife Gloria, too, which is important because Gloria's running the business now, along with her boyfriend Marco, that's another story.

"I'm Susan Summerville, the last wife!" Susan used to

introduce herself to everybody, laughing, winking, she was beautiful, and famous for that wink. Everybody always felt better when Susan walked into a room. It was kind of a gift that she had. Before he knew it, Herbert Atlas became a major art collector of Haitian art and wildlife paintings by Walton Ford and also a patron of the arts in Jacksonville, with two tuxedos and the new wing of the museum named after himself and Susan. Who woulda thunk it? Roxana would have laughed her head off. "Aw Herbie," she would have said. Soon Herb owned a Lincoln touring car, a little Mercedes sedan, and the Porsche Carrera, which his whole family made fun of, everybody except Susan, who thought he ought to have whatever he wanted. She said he'd earned it. She was teaching him how to enjoy himself. Herb owned two houses in Jacksonville; a condominium (Susan called it a "flat," wink wink) on Park Avenue in New York City, her idea; a house in Key West (her idea, too, but he loved it, what a fucking weird, crazy town!); and then another house in Key West, the big house on Washington Street. He'd bought her a little gallery down on Green Street across from Turtle Kraals. Susan enjoyed everything, and she had taught, or tried to teach, him to enjoy it, too. She used to wear these big mirror sunglasses and this bright blue silk scarf around her hairdo when he took her out driving in the Porsche with the top down. She looked like a million bucks, like a movie star. He wore a Panama hat. People actually took pictures of them when they drove down Duval Street, Herb got a real kick out of that.

And then look. Look what happened.

Early onset.

Which comes on a lot faster than regular.

Herb noticed right away, lotsa little things, but he didn't say nothing to nobody, not until he had to. He knew, though. And he took care of her, he took great care of her, because Susan (that long-legged beauty, that classy dame), she had given him a whole new life. And she was what? Only fifty-eight years old when this started happening? So now she's seventy and he's eighty-three, plenty old enough to kick the bucket anytime himself, but he's healthy. Plenty healthy, old goat. Which just goes to show you there is no God up there, no God at all, or if there is one, He's a total jerk, so fuck Him. First it was little things, the way Susan started losing her keys all the time, her purse, her sweaters, her phone, nothing bad but she never used to lose anything, she was the most organized woman he'd ever known, a businesswoman for God's sake. When she lost her goddamn Hermès watch, he didn't say a thing about it, just went out to Rite-Aid and bought her a new watch, a Timex, he was getting the picture. And she loved the Timex, she couldn't tell the difference.

She had always been a gourmet cook, but then she just sort of quit cooking, even making coffee. One morning he'd heard the funny gurgling noise and went in the big gourmet kitchen to see the coffeemaker, nothing fancy, that same damn simple kind of coffeemaker they'd had for years, bubbling over and spitting grinds and coffee and water all over the counter and the floor while Susan, his beautiful Susan, stood crying and watching it, pressing a dishtowel to her mouth. She looked lost, frightened. Herb understood. She had forgotten how to use it. He put his arms around her. "Hey, don't you worry, it's broken, we'll get you another one, dime a dozen, am I right? Come on, cheer up. Get dressed." He took her to the Banana Cafe for breakfast and by then she was smiling, laughing, charming everybody in the place. So Herb started making the coffee. They went out more and he also hired a cook, Maria, who brought dinners four days a week.

And then she really started to change. She stopped being the life of the party and just sat smiling more often than not, sometimes looking from face to face as if puzzled, answering questions but not bringing anything up. Sometimes at home she didn't speak at all but sat quietly in that solarium, which she loved, and it was like clouds were passing across her face. He used to sit there, too, on the flowered settee, holding her hand. She became more beautiful than ever, like Sleeping Beauty. It would break your goddamn heart. Herb loved her more than ever then, more than he had thought it was possible to love anybody in this world. He knew he had her on borrowed time. She'd had one accident (fender bender on the corner of Simonton and Truman), but he hadn't had the heart to take the car keys. She continued driving her little Mercedes, doing some errands, trips to the beauty salon, the post office.

Then the policeman called him from Fausto's market to say that a woman claiming to be his wife was there, she's safe, don't worry, but she says she does not know how to get home. Are you the husband? And what is your full name, sir? And what is your address, please? No, no, stay there. We're bringing her home to you. We'll bring her home, sir. Yes sir. You stay there, sir.

So Susan came riding home with two cops in a squad car like a princess, like the princess she was, smiling and apparently surprised to see Herb. "Why, hello darling!" and thanking the police effusively, wink wink, stepping carefully out of the cop car, long legs first, Jesus Christ.

"She's a doll, ain't she?" the boss cop said.

"Yes," Herb said. "Yes, she is," but that was the end of the road, the end of Susan driving herself anyplace, which was okay with Herb, he didn't mind, what else did he have to do? He was right here all the time to take her wherever she needed to go, which was primarily to the doctor by then, make that plural, the doctors by then, Jesus Christ. Though he knew. He knew before he took her the first time, before they told him. Things changed then. The big trips stopped. Maria started working full time, did all the shopping, too. Herb did everything else. Everything, got it? He wouldn't have it any other way, though he finally buckled under and brought the Home Health women in at night, the kids got on his case so bad, and now the women came full time. Okay. But all in all Herb could still sing that Frank Sinatra song, "I Did It My Way," about his whole damn life, maybe he's not proud of some things in his life now, some things involving women, but he's not gonna go there, because he's proud of this thing, Susan. He's done good by Susan, he's done all right.

But somebody's touching his shoulder. "Yeah? Yeah?" Herb pushes himself up straight in the breakfast nook, clutching his pajama bottoms. "Sorry." It's that girl Renee, she's hypnotized Herb, too. She giggles, puts a hand up to her snaggletooth. Who the hell is this girl?

"All done," she says. "Come see." She's got her bags and stuff all packed up, ready to go. She touches his sleeve so he hauls himself out of the breakfast nook and goes over there to the bay window and damn if Susan isn't sleeping like a baby now, all lolled back in the big chair, feet up and stretched out before her on the matching hassock. Herb does a double take. Damn. This girl has painted Susan's toenails a bright rosy pink and put some little sparkly thing like a diamond in the middle of each toenail. What the fuck?

"Ssssh," the girl says, seeing his face. "She likes it."

The girl leans over to tuck Susan's robe around her more closely, then pats Susan's folded hands. Susan stirs, some expression crossing her face, or almost. She almost looks like herself again for a minute. Damn. Herb leans forward. Susan opens her eyes and looks directly at him for a moment, his old Susan, she knows him. She *knows* him. Something like an electric shock goes through Herb's whole body. God, he loves her. Then she sighs and closes her eyes again and she is gone. Shaken, Herb stands back.

The girl is all packed up and ready to go, now she's stretching or doing yoga or something, hands above her head, and this is when Herb notices it, her rack, as the guys used to say back in the day. How come this girl is doing pedicures? This is a waste of talent. She oughta be working at Hooters.

"All done?" bossy Pat calls softly from the door. "How'd it go? The next home health nurse is already here, she's been waiting."

"Ssssh." Renee puts her finger to her mouth and they go out as the new girl goes in, the three of them now in the gazebo garden just beyond the door, where Renee says the ingrown toenail wasn't so bad, really, she thinks it will be okay now. "I fixed it. You have to cut toenails straight across," she announces. Pat and Herb just nod.

"Can you take a card?" Pat asks, taking over the way she does. "Or a check?" Apparently the price has been agreed on.

"Oh no," the girl says, with a worried little frown. "Cash only. Sorry. I hope that's not a problem."

Pat looks at Herb. "You got some cash?"

"Now, whaddya think, Pat?" Herb fumbles around with his pajamas to find the money belt, then pulls out two of the hundred dollar bills he is famous for. He hands it to the girl. "Keep the change, honey. Whatever you did, it was worth every penny."

"Oh my goodness!" the girl says in surprise, opening her big sparkly purse then dropping it on the paving stones. She kneels down to pick everything up, then gives a little wave as she leaves.

"You gotta go in there and look at Susan," Herb says. "Honest to God, she's all relaxed, she's sleeping like a baby right now. You won't believe it. We gotta get that girl back, she's like magic or something."

Pat smiles at him, always a bad sign. "Great idea, Herb. I'm glad this was helpful. Maybe she does massages, too. But you know, Maribeth and I agree. Everybody agrees. Susan ought to be in a facility now. You've been lucky, but this has gone on long enough. You're running a house of cards here."

Herb chooses to ignore her. "So call that girl again. Renee. Let's get her back over here for a massage or whatever, her and her two friends." When Pat turns to stare at him quizzically, he makes push-up motions at his chest, like he's pushing up big breasts.

"Herb, you may be old, but you're still disgusting. Truly disgusting. You've got no filter at all." But she's smiling, Pat, she can't help it, the old dyke, shaking her dykey head as she slips inside the guest wing to check on Susan herself.

Herb checks his money belt, then leans over to investigate something shiny he can just glimpse under the frilly edge of a fern, on the paving stones. The girl's wallet. Damn. He retrieves it and then hitches up his pajama bottoms and charges across the garden, into the house, and across the solarium, past the ugly as hell Chihuly glass sculpture, and into the vestibule, where he throws open the big door to shout, "Renee! Renee! You left your wallet, honey."

He's almost too late. She's already out on the street, nearly gone, but she hears him. She's turning around now. On impulse, almost like a reflex, Herb opens the wallet and looks at some kind of ID picture, which shows her with a much thinner face, long brown hair, no smile. Deirdre June Mullins, Mountain Home School, Pineville, NC.

She drops her bags and comes running down the walk, ponytail flipping from side to side.

He holds the wallet out to her.

"Oh my goodness!" she says, grabbing it, giving him a big smile. "Thanks so much, Mr. Atlas."

"Sure thing, honey. See you next time." Herb steps out the door and stands on the stoop to watch her go all the way down Washington Street, out of sight.

Tree House

I swear, it was all I could do to keep from skipping all the way down Washington Street, skipping just like me and Martha used to do coming up the holler after the school bus let us off up home, skipping and jumping for joy with two hundred-dollar bills just burning a hole in my purse, and plenty more where that came from. I know a good thing when I see it, and I was going to jump right on this one! That poor sick lady and that wild old man, they needed me. They had got a bad situation over there and I was the girl for the job. I'm real good at making people feel better even though Paula said I had to get over that and just think about what was good for Dee Dee. Well I thought, this is good for Dee Dee for sure! I could just see myself going to that big pink house again and again, giving everybody over there manicures and massages, whatever they want, I could just say I'm a trained massage therapist, why not? Anybody can rub on people and make them feel better. Old people just like to be touched anyhow, nobody ever touches them anymore because they have gotten so old and icky.

I crossed Simonton and then all of a sudden I wanted to see Willie so bad I couldn't stand it. So I checked my watch and saw I had four hours before my next appointment, which was on Windsor Circle anyhow, not so far from the Tree House, so instead of going back to the trailer I hopped on the bus in front of Rite Aid and headed over that way, I just couldn't help it.

I got off on Truman and then went down Poor House Lane, which gets littler and littler until you get to the house where Willie lives down at the very end, all grown over with vines and flowers and almost hidden behind the biggest trees you have ever seen, banyan trees, it's a real jungle, you might find anything in there! So I went down the walk and turned right past the long porch with its old Christmas wreath still hanging on the door and tinsel on the railings and a jumble of old furniture left everywhichaway like crazy people had been out there having a party, which is probably true. It's not really a tree house but a big old fancy house like a castle from the olden days when everybody was rich, now it's all been cut up into apartments. I followed the weird little path around the house and through the garden, or what used to be the garden I guess, walking on these stepping-stones that look like moons and sunflowers and cat faces, some sculptor made them, several artists have their studios here, Willie said.

I opened the side door, which was never locked, and went up the dark stairs to the third floor, really dragging my ass by then because I was still carrying all my stuff, and finally turned the knob on Willie's door. A blue door. Sky blue. Some lady artist lived here and did all this wild painting, each wall a different color, lime green, pink, yellow, you never saw anything like it.

"Surprise!" I hollered. Willie was laying on a big mattress on the floor turned toward the long doors onto the deck. The deck sticks right out into the middle of the biggest banyan tree of all, entirely surrounded by thick, leathery leaves, which close it in and rustle all the time up here in a breeze you can't even feel down below, throwing these random spots of sunshine all over the deck and all over Willie on the mattress with papers and books spread out all around him, kind of like a boy on a raft or a boy from some other time and place, I always think this. Willie reads so many books, he's like a boy in a book himself. He sat up on the mattress and took off his big black glasses real careful and then held his arms out with that lopsided grin and I dropped everything on the floor with a bang and went right over there pulling my clothes off on the way.

"It's a miracle!" he cried. "I was just thinking about you and now you're here! I thought you had to work, I can't believe you're here!" His whole face lit up. Despite all those big books he reads, Willie is just like a child, or like somebody who has been left to grow up all alone out in the woods and lived on berries and talked to the animals like a wild boy on the Discovery Channel. I'm not kidding. Willie doesn't ever watch TV for instance, he doesn't even own a TV and he doesn't even know what *Survivor* is, or anything. He loves plants and trees and the out-of-doors, he runs around all over Key West in his cutoffs and those old red tennis shoes with his long hair flying out behind him like a flag. He is real tall and thin, but not exactly skinny. It's like he's running in slow motion, his legs are so long. Like a giraffe or something. People turn to stare, I've seen them do it.

I got a running start myself and jumped right on top of him.

I feel like I've been with Willie all my life but in truth I just met him three weeks ago, on a Tuesday, which has always been a lucky day for me. I met him in the Margaret-Truman Drop-off Launderette on Truman Avenue where he was putting his clothes in all wrong and didn't even have a clue how to work the washer, you could tell he had never done this before in his whole life. I got real tickled, watching him while my own wash was whirling around. He kept struggling to open this little packet of detergent he had got out of the vending machine until finally I got up and went over there and said, "You don't have to open that up, silly! Looky here!" I grabbed it. "You just stick the whole thing in here, like this."

"But what about that plastic?" he asked, grinning, and so I said, "That plastic is going to melt in the water, silly, don't you know anything?"

"Well, I guess I don't, for a fact." He watched as I reached in and evened up the load—it was just jam-packed!—and then slammed down the lid and punched EXTRA LARGE LOAD and COLD WASH and got it going.

He shook his head, all those curls, like I had really done something. He acts like he was fotched up on the moon, like my granny used to say. "That's amazing."

"No it's not," I said. "Piece of cake." Something else my granny used to say.

"Well, thank you. Now can I buy you a sandwich or something, to thank you for real? Have you had lunch? We can go up the street and get some lunch."

I had to smile at that. "You can't just run off and leave your laundry like that while it's going, you know."

"You can't?" he said. "Why not?"

I pointed up at the sign, which said DO NOT LEAVE LAUNDRY UNATTENDED. "Somebody is likely to steal it if you're not here when it gets dry, is why," I said. "If you're not here, they'll just put it in their basket—or your basket—and walk off with it. They've got a whole lot of homeless people down here, and folks just down on their luck . . ."

He frowned and then grinned that big goofy grin that goes all the way across his face. "How about a Coke then?" He pointed to the Coke machine.

"Mountain Dew, please," I said, "if they've got one, or Sprite if they ain't." Then I could of cut off my tongue for saying *ain't*, which I am trying to remember not to do.

"Yes ma'am." He crossed over to the drink machine in three long steps and came back with a Mountain Dew for me, a bottle of water for him, and we sat down across from the washing machines on these orange plastic chairs just like anybody, I will never forget it.

"I'm Willie. Now tell me your name," he said right off, and I said "Dee Dee," which surprised me so much I liked to fell off of my seat, for I had gotten so good at never ever giving it out, making up other names for my own protection.

"That sounds Southern," he said, and I allowed as to how it *was* Southern, but then I said I was from Tennessee instead of North Carolina. When he said, "What brought you down here?" I told him that I had just left an abusive relationship in Miami and came to Key West to get a new lease on life. He looked real serious at that and said he was so sorry. "What a terrible thing to go through," he said. "I don't see how anybody could be mean to you, he must have been a monster."

"Well, it wasn't really his fault," I heard myself going right on, since I hated to make my made-up fiancé *too* bad, I mean there is a reason why most folks go off the tracks, so I said it was PTSD, that he had just served two tours in Afghanistan. "It was real bad over there. He couldn't help what he did, he just went crazy is all. It was real sad." I almost believed it myself.

Willie nodded gravely, sympathetic. "So you're just visiting, then? Or do you actually live here?"

"I live here right now," I said. "But I can get a job anyplace, anytime."

"What do you do?"

"I'm an aesthetician," I said.

He sat up. "But what do you actually *do*?"

"Nails," I said. "Manicures and pedicures. I can work for myself, or in a salon or with an agency like I'm doing right now. What about you?"

He smiled a big smile that melted my heart. "I guess you might say I'm an aesthetician too."

"What?"

"A different kind of aesthetician. I'm just visiting down

here this semester, taking some time off from graduate school."

"What kind of a school is that?" I asked.

He smiled. "Any kind you want," he said. "If you want to learn more after college."

"Well, what are you learning, then?"

"That's a damn good question, honey." He laughed. "Sometimes I wonder myself. Religion. Art history. Philosophy. Mostly I'm just reading, I guess, and writing some poetry. And thinking. Some people might say I'm running away, but I believe I'm somewhere I need to be. So it's a good time. A necessary time."

"Huh" was all I could think of to say to that. I got it, though. So he was a geek, then, a sweet-as-hell, honest-to-god geek, not a thing like any of the guys I had ever known, and I felt myself letting my guard down enough to give him my cell phone number when he asked even though I knew I was not supposed to do that unless it was a trusted friend. That's what Paula had said, *a trusted friend,* but even though I had only known him about an hour and half by then, I felt like he was. So we just kept on talking and talking and then the clothes got dry and we folded them all up and carried them back outside into that blinding sunlight and I felt so hot and exposed and lonely all of a sudden standing out there on the sidewalk holding my laundry basket. Then he stuck out his hand in a sweet, geeky way and I dropped my laundry basket and shook it, and then we went off our separate ways and it was like the bottom had just dropped out of the whole world until about twenty minutes later when my phone rang and it was him

asking me did I want to go down to the Mallory dock tomorrow night to see the sunset and then get something to eat.

"Do what?" I said and he laughed and explained how it is
a big tourist thing in Key West to go down to the public dock
at the end of Duval Street and watch the sun go down, it's
kind of like a carnival at sunset every night. So he was asking
me for a date! Which I have not hardly ever had, believe it or
not, and so of course I said yes though I had never heard of
such a date as that.

WE MET AT the big clock in Mallory Square and I felt stupid
because I had gotten just a little bit dressed up, I had put on
my blue sequin top and high-heeled sandals and I could see
immediately that this was not the place. But then I realized
that it didn't matter, people were wearing every damn thing
in the world and some of them practically nothing! We were
surrounded by the craziest people I have ever seen in my life,
hundreds of them it seemed, dancers and singers and jugglers
and one guy that was a sword swallower, I swear! It did not
look like a trick either, the sword just disappeared down his
neck. I was real close to him when he did this. And another
guy had a bunch of trained cats, I mean plain old house cats,
jumping through hoops and the like. I had already been in
Key West for almost a month and I didn't know nothing—I
mean *anything*!—about all this. I swear, you could have got
papers on just about all of those people. And hanging over the
top of the whole thing was that great big red sun itself, sink-
ing faster and faster the lower it got in the sky, people getting
quieter now and bunching together or holding hands—by

then *we* were holding hands!—as it got closer and closer to
the waterline, the *horizon* Willie called it, and then everybody
was yelling and cheering when it finally touched the horizon
all spread out like a beehive and then boom it was gone, just
disappeared the way everything does, just plain gone, and I
started crying like crazy. I don't know why and I was real
embarrassed but he brushed my tears away with his hand and
said, "I knew I liked you." All around us, people were still
looking at the horizon and Willie told me they were looking
for the green flash and I said "What?" through my tears and
he said, "If you see a green flash right after the sun goes down,
it means good luck. Did you see it?" he asked me, squeezing
my shoulder, and I had to smile at that and say, "Not hardly."

Then we got hot dogs and sat on the stone wall down at
the water's edge to eat them and then he said, "Hey, wanna go
back to the Tree House with me?" and I said, "What is that?"
And he said the Tree House was where he lived. So he got us
a pedicab! Which I had never ridden in in my life, sitting so
high above the street full of people, the driver wore a top hat
and there was a pink feather on the horse's harness. I used to
love horse books when I was a little girl, Black Stallion books
and *Misty of Chincoteague*, I got them from the bookmobile
and had forgotten all about it until right then. The bookmobile stopped at the mouth of the holler every Tuesday morning
in the summertime. I was always down there waiting with
the book I had read, just dying to get a new one. The pedicab
went through the crowds up Duval and then out Eaton Street
till we got over there close to the cemetery. It was a long ride
and then he was pulling lots of bills out of his wallet to pay

the guy. I said to myself, *This boy is either real rich or real poor*, but I could not tell which for the life of me. Then we walked on to the Tree House and Willie used his cellphone for a flashlight as we went around the side through all those scary black bushes and up the little stairs, which scared me, too. For a minute I was thinking, *Well what have you gone and got yourself into now after everything else you have been through?* And I was afraid I was going to blow it, all of it, but that was wrong, he was just a boy that lived in a crazy tree house, like Peter Pan or Robin Hood or somebody, and I realized that he was like that on purpose, which made it okay. It really was like he had grown up on the moon.

That first time on the mattress I could tell he didn't know anything, I mean nothing. Then he touched me all over real slow like I was something new in the world, something to be prized, and so I was. "Oh my god, oh my god," he said over and over. And then we just laid there laughing while that whole mattress filled up with random moving pieces of moonlight shining through the rustling leaves of the banyan tree, it was like being in a light show at a concert. It was like being in an old movie, a "silent film," Willie said. I swear I will never pass by another banyan tree in my life without thinking about it. I stayed that whole night and then he called a cab and sent me home the next morning in plenty of time for me to get cleaned up and make it to my next job at 10 a.m.

So, *rich* is what I think he is now. Maybe real rich. And I think he really likes me, too. Me, Dee Dee!

First Honeymoon

This is the silk scarf from Venice
So new so nice
Good to touch
Now this is the silk scarf from Venice
Gold and red
Slick and soft
At the window
I wear only the scarf
The curtains fall down to the floor
Pools of silk
Oh see the piazza
See the flags and the fountain blowing
Gondolas pierce the canal like fish
The man behind me is my husband
I have a husband!
Louis
You say Lou-eee

Black curls, black eyes
Black hair all over his back
What a handsome devil, someone said
I was so young
Was I ever that young?
Louis was never young
Old soul
Bayou soul
From the boot of Louisiana
He comes up behind me
The scarf slides to the floor
I love you, I love you
I love you

"Damn, you hear that? Hey, baby, I love you, too!" Herb almost falls, rushing over to stand in front of her chair.

Susan opens her eyes—those wide, golden cat's eyes. She holds out her arm toward him, thin hand drooping from thin wrist. "I don't believe I have had the pleasure," she says formally but with the old lilt, her old classy manners.

Renee puts her hand to her mouth, laughing, the way she does, and even Herb has got to chuckle at that one. Then Susan smiles, actually smiles.

"I'll be damned! Now she's smiling, look at that!" Herb wishes that Pat and Maribeth and Ashley and everybody else who's been giving him so much shit about the goddamn nursing home was here right now this very minute, but of course they're not, they're off someplace else living their own goddamn lives while they tell him how to run his. "I tell you what, honey, you're a jewel, you know that?"

Renee smiles. "I think she likes to come outside," she says.

"Yeah, well, who knew? Whoever took the goddamn trouble to get her out here? Or dress her up a little?"

This afternoon Renee has got Susan wearing a soft blue silk robe. Renee stands behind her, massaging Susan's thin back and shoulders until the gathering clouds fill her mind and obscure the garden before her, the yellow roses, the pansies with their little smiles, the white lilies, the pink bougainvillea just blooming its crazy head off.

Letter to Paula

Dear Paula,

I guess you are suprised to hear from me after what I did, but I think of you every single day of my life, I will never forget you and how good you were to me and all the things you told me. I know you are dissapointed in me but there was a good reason for Tamika and me taking off like that tho I can not tell you what happened, it was not your fault. You have a good program and you taught us a lot and we are okay. I have got a real nice job doing nails at old people homes and rich peoples houses! And Tamika is a waitress at the IHOP and a nice man has just up and give us a little trailer to stay in for free, it is pink, and round on top like a loaf of bread and just like a doll house inside with everything little, I love it, it is the onlyest place of my own I ever had you know, I have always lived with other people so this is real nice only me and Tamika. We are like Princesses here, remember when we used to sing the Princess songs for you? And Tamika was Belle and I was Ariel the little mermaid with red hair or sometimes we would switch around and sometimes we would both be Tiana, remember how much we loved to sing that song, "Down in New Orleans"? Remember how good Tamika can sing those Tiana songs? May be we really will get to Disney World now and see all those real Princesses and Tamika and me will get a job singing THERE. Well you have to dream, remember when you said that? You always said DREAM BIG. Remember when we used to sit on the fire escape at the program and the stars was so big and so close I will never forget it. I will never forget you. I just wanted you to know that Tamika and me are fine and guess what? I have got a real boy friend now too, he is sweet and smart and loves me, me Dee Dee. I feel like I am a Princess now for sure whether we ever get to Disney World or not.

So love from me Dee Dee!

P.S. You will be proud to know that I have got me a vocabulary book now to improve myself, it is right here
My boyfriend is a poet
He is GENEROUS (word)
And COORDINATED (word)
And HIRSUTE (word)
Ha ha! Dee Dee!

House Money

Ricky's already parked and waiting for him out there on Washington Street in front of the house, driving the old red Chevy convertible, he calls it a classic, *ha*! Piece of shit. Herb believes in the newest, the best. He doesn't get this classic shit. But Ricky likes his cars old and his clothes old and even his musical instruments old, too, such as the prize Martin guitar and those old horns he buys in New Orleans and Chicago. Ricky has been stylin' and profilin' what he calls it, ever since he was a boy. And he's got a real look, that rich brown skin, the porkpie hat, Susan always said he was an artist, a street artist, a genius. Susan loved Ricky the minute she met him and she continued to know who he was longer than she recognized anybody else, even her own kids, go figure. Anyhow Herb bought Ricky this Chevy himself back in the day, back when Ricky was in high school in Jacksonville, back when Herb was married to Ricky's mama, Gloria Estevez, who used to work for him, now what a piece of work *she* was! Big, curvy woman. Big brain, smart as a whip—too smart, too young for him! But since Gloria had left her first husband, Stan—the bodybuilder—for Herb, maybe Herb shouldn't have been surprised when she left him, too, for this young computer dude, a nerd, a geek really. T-Boy—not even a name! Old blue jeans and a black T-shirt, that's the only clothes he's got, this T-Boy who's running the company now with Gloria and Mario, Herb's nephew, they're doing a damn good job of it, too, though Herb doesn't understand half of what they're doing, it's all on the internet or it's up in the iCloud, whatever. Which doesn't mean a goddamn thing to Herb—it's out there in the air somewhere, what the hell. You gotta roll with the punches. Who woulda thunk it?, as his own sweet, sainted Roxana used to say back in Buffalo, back in the day, oh Jesus.

As for Ricky, once he got into that summer program for teens up at Berklee in Boston, he never looked back. When he does visit Florida now, for a gig or whatever, he stays in Key West, not with his mom and T-Boy up in Jacksonville. Hell, Susan had fixed up a whole apartment over the garage here just for him with what she called a forties décor, wink wink—leopard rug, big mirrors, great sound system, vintage jazz posters, little deck with a hot tub, and the old Chevy right there in the four-car garage below, for whenever Ricky showed up. Which he has now. Actually Herb thinks one of the other kids must have gotten in touch with Ricky, such as Maribeth or Pat, what a busybody, or even Ashley. But boy is Herb glad to see him now.

Ricky is the best of them all in Herb's opinion, the whole

bunch of them, all his kids and half-kids, the whole coalition, the Rainbow Coalition is what Herb calls them though nobody even knows what that means anymore, and come to think about it, Herb may have forgotten himself! It was from the eighties though, he thinks. An eighties thing. People of every color and background.

Ricky is the one who put the rainbow in the Rainbow Coalition, Gloria had him in high school in Miami. "My sweet love child!" she always called him, and never one word—not one!—about who the daddy might be or where he was. "This is *my* baby," she used to say, doting on him, Gloria and her mama and her aunts all doting on him. Shit! No wonder Ricky grew up thinking he's God's gift to women.

"Hey man!" Ricky jumps out of the red car now and bounds across the yard to envelop Herb in the biggest hug in the world, grizzling him with the dreads and the beard. He holds Herb out at arm's length to announce, "Well, shit, you look just the same to me, man."

"Who's been telling you any different?" Herb growls at him.

Ricky spreads his arms wide, shrugging in the Hawaiian shirt. "Don' nobody tell me nothing, mon," he says in the island patois he likes to affect in Key West. "Me I gotta gig at the Gardens Hotel tonight. So here I am. Where we goin' today? You tell me, mon."

"Ah—hold on just a minute." Herb disappears behind a giant flowering azalea. "All the time, man," Herb says, coming out of the azalea now, zipping up. "All the goddamn time,

I'm telling you. That's where we're going today," he says as Ricky opens the passenger door for him.

"Where? The bathroom?" Ricky cracks himself up.

"Shit no." Herb takes the card out of his shirt pocket and reads it out loud. "202 North Roosevelt Boulevard. Out on the Gulf by the Navy Base."

"So what's up?" Driving, Ricky lounges way back, exactly like he did in high school. Slow jazz blooms out of the dashboard.

"Nothin's up, that's part of the problem," Herb says and then has to join in Ricky's big laugh. "Yeah, that and the peeing and some other stuff, too. But I'm gonna consult the doctor, not you."

"Maybe you oughta consult me, though," Ricky says. "I can get you a mojo hand." Ricky lives in New Orleans most of the time.

"Yeah, well, get me one, then. I could use it." Herb does not tell Ricky about the blood in his urine or the aches and pains he's got all over his body these days, probably got nothing to do with any of this other shit anyhow. And his dick? The famous dick that's gotten Herb in trouble all his life? He hasn't even seen it for years, belly's too big. So *somebody* had better take a look at it, that's what Herb figures.

THINGS HAVE CHANGED considerably since Herb last visited the doctors' office in the big medical building out here on Roosevelt Avenue, Herb sees this right away. For one thing, they've got the building all jazzed up with a fancy entrance like it's a hotel or something. And the nurses have quit wearing white nurse uniforms, now they're all wearing pajamas apparently. A pretty redhead in green pajamas comes over to take his arm like he's an old man or something. Ricky gives her a big smile and then vanishes. So the nurse sits Herb down in the waiting room, where they've got ESPN on the big television, water skiing, that's not even a sport for Christ's sake, and nothing to read either except O, *The Oprah Magazine* and AARP. Fuck AARP. Then another nurse, a bigger one with a spiky haircut and glasses, comes to get him and takes him into a little room where she basically bombards him with shit, all these paper forms to fill in. Her nametag says Diane McCutcheon.

"Whoa, hold on a minute here," Herb says. "All I wanna do is see the doctor for a minute. I've got a couple questions for him."

"*Mister Atlas*," she begins severely. "We see by your records that you have not been in for almost four years, not even for a physical. Is that correct?"

"Yeah, well, I've been kind of busy," Herb says.

"Busy?" She looks at him over the glasses. "It says here that you have been retired since—" She consults his chart.

"Yeah, well, there's other work besides work. My wife Susan, she's got Alzheimer's."

"Oh, I'm so sorry!" The nurse changes her tune. "So what has finally brought you to in to see us today, Mr. Atlas?"

"Urine," he says. "Getting up all night. Running behind a potted plant at the mall. I've got a personal knowledge of every damn restroom and potted plant in Key West. Nobody ever told me that this was gonna happen."

Finally she smiles at him, writing on his chart. "Other issues? Any leaking? Any pain or burning during urination? Any blood in the urine?"

"Yeah."

"Yes what? Or which?"

"All of it, honey. All of the above. I'm guilty for all of the above."

She's writing. She looks up to ask, "Erectile dysfunction?"

"Are you kidding me, honey? I'm eighty-three years old, I weigh two hundred and thirty-five pounds, of course I've got erectile dysfunction."

"You should have come in sooner, Mr. Atlas," she says, mouth in a thin line.

"Are you kidding me? The way I look at it, honey, I'm doing okay. For my age, I'm doing just fine. I've lived for eighty-three years, I'm playing with house money now." He sees that she doesn't get it. She probably doesn't even know what "house money" is.

"Other problems?" she continues, relentless. "Aches, pains, depression?"

"Yep," he says. "Sure. All the time."

"The last time you were here, you were treated for atrial fibrillation," she announces as if she has caught him out in a lie or something.

"Yeah, that's right. And I've got a little pacemaker right in here right now, doing its little job."

"Your medications are metoprolol, omeprazole, rosuvas-tatin, losartan . . ." She reels off a bunch of them. "You are still taking these medications, correct?"

"Yeah," he says, though the truth is that he takes them when he remembers, and sometimes he forgets. He must be getting enough, though, since that little guy in his chest has been quiet for a good long while. "I tell you what, though. Fibrillation is a damn funny thing."

She looks at him over her glasses. "What do you mean?"

"Well, everybody's doing it, for one thing, every other old guy I know." Herb leans back in his chair. "It's very popular. Fibrillation is sort of like having a roommate who never said anything and now he starts talking all the damn time. So it's like, hey, who *is* this guy?"

Finally! A big laugh, a real laugh out of Nurse Ratchett. "Well, I must say, you have certainly spiced up my morning, Mr. Atlas. Now if I can just trouble you with a few more of our required forms?"

"Sure, sweetie, but I've gotta pee something terrible first. You oughta know that by now."

"Oh, of course. Just down the hall to your left."

After he pees (blood, yeah; pain, yeah), Herb considers leaving, just walking out the door right now. But shit, he's got Susan to think about, all the time. All the damn time. He's gotta get this stuff fixed.

"So what else you got for me, honey?" He says as he sits back down heavily.

The nurse has placed a glossy booklet in front of him, it looks like a magazine, with some old dude and some old woman all dressed up and hugging each other in front of a blooming rosebush on the cover. Pink roses. They look happy, but this is a fake. The booklet is entitled *Medical Care Decisions and Advance Directives.*

Shit. Herb knows what this is about.

Diane McCutcheon is already doing her spiel. "Now I assume that you have already made these decisions, Mr. Atlas." She leafs through the booklet, reading out loud, stuff like "My Living Will, Health Care Power of Attorney, and Advance Directive for a Natural Death."

"Whoa! Wait a minute." Herb holds up his hand. "I'm not going there, honey. I'm not gonna do this bullshit."

She eyes him severely. "That would be very irresponsible, Mr. Atlas."

And what fucking business is it of yours? He does not say. Instead he says, "Thanks, honey, I'll take it along home with me then, give it a look."

Relieved, Diane places it in a clear plastic pouch, taking out yet another form with a long list of Daily Activities on one side and the question, "Are you able to perform these activities without help?" on the other. Herb runs his eyes down the list of activities, which read:

Drinking
Eating
Cleaning
Driving
Shopping
Going to the Toilet

He looks up. "Are you kidding me?"

"No, absolutely not. Please fill in the blank for each activity on a scale of one to four, one would be no difficulty, two would be very little difficulty, three would be some difficulty, and four would mean, 'I always need help.'"

"I get it, I get it." Herb dispenses with this fast, all ones, though that's not true for any of them.

"Just one more." Now Diane places a square blank piece of paper in front of him.

He looks at her. "So what's this? A trick question?"

"We want you to draw a clock, please, sir. A clock that shows the time at seven-fifteen." Diane hands him a black marker, taking off the top.

"You've got to be kidding me, honey. You're pulling my leg."

"Absolutely not."

"Come on now. Who couldn't do that?"

"Lots of people. You wouldn't believe the things we get." She grins at him.

Feeling challenged, Herb grabs the marker and pulls the paper toward himself, drawing a big black circle on the page. He puts a dot in the middle of the circle, then pauses, in a sudden panic. *Shit.* Where do those numbers start? And which way do they run? Actually this is kind of a trick, isn't it? He's had nothing but digital clocks for years, that's the problem. That's what makes it so hard. But finally it comes to him. He makes a black 12 at the top of his circle, a 6 at the bottom, then quickly fills in the rest. Okay. Then another long pause for the hands of the clock, like arrows, little and big. 7:15.

"Piece of cake." He shoves the paper across the table, back to Diane.

She smiles a sort of superior smile, then stands up. "Very good. Good job, Mr. Atlas." She says it like he's in kindergarten.

"What? No more games?"

"You may see the doctor now. Please follow me." *Nice ass, after all*, Herb thinks as they walk single file down a long hall with pictures of tropical flowers all along it, like a gallery, reminding him of Susan. Everything reminds him of Susan. The nurse stops before the next to last door, knocks, then opens it. "This is Rebecca Hughes, Dr. Shapiro's nurse," she announces. "And this is Herbert Atlas. He's quite the character, so watch out!"

"Wait a minute there," Herb protests, but this new nurse, a skinny blonde, just laughs and hands him a white gown.

"So where's the goddamn doctor? I'm here to see a doctor." Now Herb is fed up.

Both nurses smile. "Good luck, sir," the first one says, leaving.

"Dr. Shapiro will be here just as soon as you're ready," the new one says. "Take off all your clothing including your shoes and put this gown on, opening in the front, please. Just knock on the door when you're ready." And she's gone.

"Well shit." Now Herb remembers why he doesn't go to the doctor, how much he hates it. It takes him a long time to undress, just like it takes him a long time to dress every day. Well the goddamn doctor will just have to wait. Finally he's ready, completely naked as the day he was born, nothing but Herbert under the gown. He's exhausted by the time he knocks on the door, which opens immediately to admit Nurse Rebecca and the doctor.

"Good morning, Mr. Atlas! Congratulations! The nurses and I thought you drew the best clock we've seen all week." Smiling, radiating confidence, Dr. David Shapiro holds out his hand.

Herb can't believe it. The doctor is twelve years old.

"OH COME ON, Herb, mon!" Ricky doubles over laughing in the driver's seat. "The doctor is not twelve years old. He can't be twelve years old. First he had to go to college and then he had to go to doctor school for, like, ten years."

"Maybe he's fourteen, then." Herb leans back exhausted. He feels like he's been in one of those races, whadda they call them now? A *marathon*.

"Listen to me. That's what you want, one of these real young ones that just got out of medical school. They're the ones that know everything, all the latest stuff. They're the ones you want."

So maybe the kid's got a point. Herb looks out at the blue water and all the Jet Skis and little boats out there. Somebody's up on a Parasail. He hates everybody that's young, everybody that's having fun.

"Now what's next?" Ricky asks. "Maybe you wanna go straight to Walgreens and fill a prescription or something? You got a prescription?"

"Well, now, lemme see." Herb pretends to look at the handful of prescriptions and referral forms he's still clutching.

"Lemme see here. Just a goddamn minute. Okay. Here we go." He holds up one of the little pieces of paper. "Here's the prescription. Take one martini, dry, on the rocks immediately."

"You got it." Ricky wheels the Chevy around and heads for Louie's.

Pedicure

When Pat came in and said that Mrs. Atlas won't need me this afternoon because her daughter Ashley is coming for a visit today—Ashley is the one that lives up in Del Ray, she's a nurse or something—well I just about ran up the street to Simonton and jumped on the bus and headed straight over to the Tree House.

I am fixing to surprise him!

Now what will he be doing? I wonder. Reading or writing or running, I reckon, he don't do much else. I think about picking up a Cuban sandwich from 5 Brothers for lunch but I just can't wait that long to see him. I come tiptoeing up the stairs and turn the glass knob in the blue door r-e-a-l s-l-o-w. "Surprise!" I holler and then the awfullest thought comes into my head, what if he is up here with some other girl? What will I do then? It would just about kill me, I realize all of a sudden. It would flat-out kill me for sure.

"Baby is that you? Is it really you?" He's out on the deck in an old chair he's dragged out there, smoking a joint and writing something in a notebook. He throws it down and jumps up and grabs me. "I was just thinking about you and here you are. It's like a dream come true." He's got this big, wide smile. Charming, he is charming and winsome and princely. (words)

"I got off early," I say, kissing him. All I ever have to do is look at him and I want to kiss him. I reckon I've got it pretty bad. "So what do you want to do?" I say, thinking I know the answer to that one, but Willie can always surprise me.

He takes the last toke real slow, considering. "What I would really like to do is get a pedicure. I want to know what you do. Can you give me a pedicure? Guys have pedicures, too, don't they?"

"All the time," I tell him, "especially the old ones that can't reach their feet. And then there are some guys that get off on it, too."

"Are you kidding me? Is that really true?"

"Well, sure," I say. "Especially if you're older than dirt and your feet hurt and nobody young has touched you in about a million years. Think about it. When I worked up at Silver Lake Retirement, I had more guy clients than I could take care of. All the time. Why don't you just sit back down in that chair and relax and I'll get my kit. You just go ahead and make yourself comfortable."

By this time a lot of my nail stuff is just naturally at the Tree House since I'm staying over here so much. So I fill up the basin at the kitchen sink and get my things and a couple of towels and a pillow to get down on in front of him. He is watching me real close, very intent like. "Just relax,"

I tell him. "Take some deep, slow breaths. Count one-two-three-in, one-two-three-out. You can close your eyes if you want to."

"I don't want to," Willie says. "I want you to tell me what you're doing, baby. What's in the toolbox thing?"

So I start telling him as I lay everything out on the towel. "This is the toenail clipper. This is a nail file, to smooth the edges off after I cut them. This is the cuticle trimmer, this is a nail buffer, this is cuticle cream . . ." Then I pick up his big feet one after the other and put them down in the warm water. "Now you've got to let them soak for a little while."

"Why?"

"Well, to soften them up, so I can work on them better. So why don't you just lay back and close your eyes and I'll sing you a little song—" This works like a charm, always. Meanwhile I am examining Willie's feet, which are hard and scaly with big calluses from running around all the time and his toenails look awful from him just tearing them off whenever he gets a notion or they get to bothering him, I can tell. I massage his feet and start singing "Yesterday all my troubles seemed so far away—" and when I quit he opens his eyes and they have tears in them.

"That's beautiful," he says. If I don't watch out he's going make me cry, too.

"Thank you. But you know you really ought to take better care of your feet," I have to tell him very seriously. "It may not matter to a young man but it's going to matter a lot when you get older. They're going to give out on you if you don't take better care of them. The feet are the foundation of the body, like the foundation of a building. You might say they are the most important part of the body, in fact. Everything depends upon the feet."

"Oh is that a fact?" Now he's grinning, making fun of me.

"Yes that is a fact," I say seriously. After all, I'm a professional. "This is one thing that I know more about than you do, Mr. Smarty Pants. Why do you run so much, anyhow?" I have been wanting to ask him that for a long time. Back in the mountains where I grew up, we didn't have nobody that just ran around like that for pure-T fun. "Do you feel like you're running after something? Or away from something?"

"Now honey, that is a damn good question," Willie says, staring at me.

I lift up one foot and start to clip its nails, taking particular care with the big toe. "This is the hardest part," I explain. "You cannot round the corners down into the sides of the nail bed because the big toe is the most prone to ingrowing."

"Oh yeah?" He's still making fun of me.

"Yes sir," I say. "Not everything is in a book. You could learn a lot from me." I clip all the nails on that foot and then smooth them off with the file, and then put that foot back down in the water and start working on his other foot, which has got a big old callous on one side.

"Doesn't that hurt?" I ask, and he says it does, so I rub it down with the emery board while it's still in the water and then clip all the nails on that foot, too. Then I use my nail-brush and plain old Dawn dishwasher soap to scrub them up real good. I like Dawn better than all the fancy stuff, and it's cheaper, too.

"Well that was just great," Willie says.

"Hold your horses, we are not done yet," I tell him. I take his feet out and dry them off and put them on the green towel, the dry one, and I buff the nails with my buffer, making sure all the sharp edges are gone. "Now." I open up the lotion and work it in, toe by toe, foot by foot. "Now doesn't that feel good?" I ask him.

"Yes ma'am. And I believe it would feel even better if you took off your top," he says.

"Oh, I can't do that, sir," I say. "That wouldn't be professional. I'm an aesthetician, like I told you."

"I see," he says. "Well then, what about the polish?"

"Polish? You want polish?" I'm so surprised, men don't usually get polish. I swear, Willie is the cutest thing!

"Sure," he says. "I want everything. Everything there is to want. The whole shebang."

I get so tickled I can't do a thing but then finally I say, "Well, what color do you want, sir?"

And then Willie says, "Why don't you just surprise me, honey?" and lays back in the chair and closes his eyes and starts breathing in and out, in and out the way I showed him, 1-2-3, 1-2-3. Well, I like to died! Talk about surprising somebody! I take out my best line of OPI and set them up right there, all them little bottles like some crazy little army on the deck. Then I take a Q-tip and dip it in nail polish remover and run it over all his toenails one by one. It is very important to wipe all the excess lotion off or the polish will not adhere. Then I apply a clear base coat on every single nail. Willie don't open his eyes. He just keeps breathing in and out, in and out, 1-2-3-, 1-2-3. By then I can tell he's really asleep, so I go ahead and put polish on his nails one by one, every one a different color. Strawberry Margarita, Mexico City, Glitter Girl, Baby Pink, Plum Pretty.

Now applying the polish is much harder than anybody thinks, anybody who has not been to beauty school. Anybody who is outside the world of aesthetics, which is a pretty special little world when you get right down to it. You do not just apply a blob of polish to the nail. Too much polish and you will make a mess. What you do is paint a vertical stripe down the center of the nail, followed by another stripe on each side of the first—you try to paint all the way to the edge, but it's better to leave a little margin than to paint the skin on the side. Ridges will smooth themselves out under gravity alone. See? Looky here! Now I'm using this toothpick to get the last little bit of nail polish off.

There now! All done! I clean up the mess on the deck while Willie sleeps on, snoring his little snuffly snore, which I just love. I swear, he is more like a creature of the forest than a man. I mean, he practically lives in a tree! I finish him off with a clean top coat while he is still asleep. Then I don't know why, I just get real tickled and I've got the time, so I put some animal stencils on here and there like I use on little girls, a lion and a giraffe and a unicorn, and some sparkles and two little decals, a smiley face and a heart. The heart means I Love You. This is true.

There now. I'm done. I have to just sit back and smile at my masterpiece.

After a while, I pick his notebook up off the deck and see

that he was writing poetry when I showed up, poetry is when the lines don't go all the way across the page or make any sense. Willie writes poetry a lot and smokes dope a lot, too. I reckon they kind of go together. He thinks I have never done it, this is what I told him. Ha! Of course I have done more than that by a long shot. But I just say oh no thanks and smile and shake my head. For I am a different girl now, a new girl for Willie.

People do not have to know everything about you, Paula said. You have a right to your own private life. You can keep some things to yourself, for yourself. Every human being has the right to privacy as well as safety, she said.

So I am not about to tell Willie that I think I might have a little baby on the way. Not yet. Not till I know for sure. But I can tell you one thing. If she comes, she will be the sweetest baby in the world and I will be the best mother that ever was, me Dee Dee!

Willie sleeps on while the light changes from one side to the other, coming in through the banyan leaves, it is so beautiful up here. It is out of this world! Finally he wakes up and has a pure-T fit about his pedicure. "A real work of art!" he calls it, walking all around on the deck in and out of the random patches of sunlight. Then we are hungry, so we go out and get a big pizza and some beer at Joey's and eat every bite. But by the time we're done, the weather has changed real fast like it does all the time here, so we have to run the last little bit back to the Tree House to beat the storm, a big purple storm coming in off the ocean. We have to grab everything off the deck real fast and get it all inside just in time. Then we lay on the mattress for the rest of the evening and listen to the Avett Brothers and John Prine while Willie gets high and carries on about his pedicure—"It's a masterpiece!" he says over and over while night comes on like it does and a lot later in the night I wake up just starving and wishing I had bought that Cuban sandwich after all but there is nothing to eat here except half a box of chocolate-chip cookies so I finish that off, standing at the glass door so I can see the moon, a little old sickle moon, popping in and out, in and out of the banyan leaves, and the running clouds making a random pattern like that old-fashioned magic lantern my granny used to have.

Jewels

"Why do you say that so much?" Willie will ask her later, much later.

"What?"

"'Random.' What does it mean?"

"I don't know," she's laughing. "It kind of depends. I reckon it's just, well, random."

Still that was the prettiest thing, the changing pattern of the moonlight on the deck, she stayed up a long time to watch it and she was thinking, *I am happy I'm so happy I will remember this for the rest of my life*, and she would, too.

And so would he, William Randolph Farnsworth III— that long, strange, enchanted afternoon in the top of a banyan tree in Key West with the beautiful snaggletoothed girl who turned his toes into jewels, an afternoon set apart from the rest of his life for as long as he will live, an aesthetic and— what was that word she used all the time? An aesthetic and *random* and altogether beautiful afternoon.

Willie's Mom

One thing about the Tree House is that you always know there's other people around, coming in and out or staying there, only we just about never see any of them except for the tall skinny guy in pajamas on the porch every morning doing something called Tie Chee, which is part praying and part exercise, Willie says. But often we hear them talking or laughing real low, too low to make out the words through the yellow wall in the big room or the orange wall in the bedroom or down there on the terrace below. Well, Willie *says* it's a terrace below, but the banyan leaves cover it like a roof. Sometimes there will be a lot of voices, and a woman's high laugh, and the sound of ice clicking in a glass, or a guitar or a CD playing, or sometimes it will be a big discussion or an argument or just two voices talking like music in a conversation too soft to hear, maybe another couple, I think, a *couple*, like *us*. I'm starting to think of *us* by now, it's already been four months since I met him. Right now we're going down the stairs on our way to Pepe's for some oysters. *Raw!* Which I never ate before Willie gave me one, but I love them now, they are salty and slippery and fresh tasting and not like anything else in the world, I reckon. The word for that is *original*. Willie is real original, too, I think.

Willie opens the blue door to the pathway with me follering right along behind him and we run smack into this skinny old lady with her long white hair pulled up tight in a knot on the top of her head as awful looking as possible and a lot of makeup and real jewelry including diamond rings to die for, wearing a long muumuu type dress in a big flower print, with a manicure and a pedicure I have to admire. Very expensive. Spa stuff.

This old woman stops dead still and says, "Why William, darling, it's you, isn't it? It's really you!" She has a Southern accent and a fakey way of breathing in and out real big, *dramatic* is the word.

"Patrice." Willie bends way over like a prince to take her bony old hand and *kiss* it. I just about die.

"Oh my goodness, I thought I was lost in the jungle and what do I find but *you*, dear boy! Why I just talked to your mother a couple of days ago and she didn't even tell me you were in Key West! We're at the Marquesa, I just ran over here to find Cecil, I hear he has not been well, but I got so turned around in this crazy place, I swear it's like a real jungle in here!" She pulls back to take a good long look at Willie. "My goodness, William, you must be going native, is that it? *Native?* But I thought you were still in Cambridge."

"Oh I am," Willie says, "technically. This is just a short visit, a little retreat to clear my head, you might say."

"Indeed." Patrice gives him a long, hard look. "Well, you always were such a smart boy, I really wouldn't be surprised by anything you did, darling, and you've always marched to your own drummer, I know."

Now there were some rich old Southern ladies on the board at the program, and they were real nice. This one isn't, though, I can tell. And when Willie doesn't introduce me to her, I know something is up. He's either embarrassed about me or trying to protect me—so I go into my invisible girl thing, which I'm very good at, I've had enough practice, Lord knows. What I do is kind of hard to explain, I just fly out of my body up in the air over my head, up and up and up, and stay there as long as I need to. Sometimes I had to do this to stay alive, so I got very very good at it.

Now Patrice is talking about London and Willie has got hold of her elbow and he is kind of gently steering her along, but suddenly she stumbles on the frog steppingstone. "Well, I swear!"—she says "sway-uh"—"Oh my goodness! Oh help, help!" and he has got to really grab her and pull her up to keep her from falling flat.

"Why William!" she's shrieking now. "Why, look at your feet! Well, I nevah! I just nevah! Oh, you always were such a card. Why I'm going to call Rhoda tonight and tell her I saw you in Key West with these painted toenails, it is just too funny, who ever heard of such a thing . . . ." Patrice keeps on shrieking while Willie moves her along the pathway holding her arm like she's a real bitch on wheels while I am way way up in the sky, invisible. Then they disappear into the overgrown hedge by the street where her taxi is waiting or so she says and then they are invisible, too. I hear a car door slam, and then the engine.

"Damn it, God damn it to hell!" Willie comes crashing back through the bushes and hugs me, hard, and then I come back down and we go to Pepe's and eat oysters and get really really wasted on margaritas and he *never*, never, then or ever, mentions Patrice or his mother to me again.

But somehow I know already that she is the one—Rhoda—who put those big *R*s like a slash on the bottom of those weird paintings of flowers on the Tree House walls. She made those paintings.

All the Pretty Little Horses

It really is like Willie was fotched up on the moon, so different from me, and his mother so different from mine, it is past explaining. I think about this one night when I wake up and go in the bathroom and get a big glass of water and look at myself in the mirror by the light of the moon. It is a pure white light, but soft, like dawn. Why Dee Dee, I'm thinking, you look just like your mama now. And in the pure sweet light of the moon, I do. We could be sisters. We could sing together, a sister act.

Just the other day Miss Maribeth asked me about my own family, where are they? But I just smiled and said California. Sometimes I say Ohio. What I do not say is dead.

Paula always told us, You don't have to tell everything you know.

Old Rellar, my auntie way up on Moon Ridge, used to say, "There's tales I'll tell and tales I won't." She sat in her front parlor with her beautiful bell jar and those cards she kept shuffling and dealing over and over. Sometimes she chewed tobacco, which she spit in a brass spittoon. Old Rellar kept to herself. In fact she was dead for a long time before anybody even knew it, just sitting up there in the window of her cabin like she always did, looking down the mountain at the road. Anybody that happened to look up there would not of known she was dead.

Mama talked all the time though. If she wasn't singing, she was talking or laughing. Mama was born into a singing family way up in the mountains of Madison County, North Carolina, north of Mars Hill. I loved my mama, Lacy was her name. Her daddy played banjo with her brother on guitar and her mama played the autoharp and sang. So she grew up knowing all the old songs, the ballads that had been in their family from time memorial, as she always said. "The Cuckoo Song," "Pretty Polly," "Barbara Allen," songs about hard times and love unto death and grief never-ending. Mama could sing like a natural angel. She could even do that thing where you make your voice go up at the end of every line like a little yelp. When Mama sang the old songs, she'd put her hands behind her back and close her eyes and plant her feet real wide and firm and just let it rip. No guitar or banjo or any accompaniment.

Mama sang all around the county even as a little girl, church and tent meetings where her favorite song was "I'll Fly Away": "Oh Lordy, I'll fly away. When I get to Heaven, by and by, I'll fly away." She loved that song. Later she started going to bluegrass festivals, and that's where she met my daddy,

Billy Mullins, a boy from away, Memphis, Tennessee. Daddy played piano and slide guitar and the harmonica and sang the blues. He fell in love with the mountain music, taking down all the old songs, and then he fell in love with Mama, taking her out of the holler and down to Black Mountain near Asheville where he could get more work, tuning pianos and fixing instruments, too, and they were real happy, and she had a little boy they named Ira, and then she had me and named me Deirdre for Daddy's mother in Memphis, an old lady who came to see me when I was three months old but she stayed in Asheville in a hotel. They took me over there to meet her, and then they had me christened in the big stone church in Asheville because my grandmother insisted, the same as she had with Ira.

Mama said the preacher wore a skirt and dipped a pink rose into holy water and sprinkled it all over my face and made me cry. So I know it's crazy but sometimes even now I think I can remember that, the high arches and the candle lights and the golden cross, but maybe I just think that because of my mama telling me about it so much, over and over. Mama used to laugh and say, "You don't have to worry Dee Dee, you will never go to Hell because you got double baptized," baptized in that big church in Asheville and then in the running water of Home Creek. The old-time Baptists think it's got to be running water or it doesn't count.

My family never did go to church regular that I can recall, for my daddy did not really believe in it, and so Mama didn't, either. She thought the sun rose and set on Billy, and wrote a beautiful song about him, named "City Boy." My brother Ira looked just like Daddy, and Daddy taught him how to sing and dance, too, flatfoot and clog, on a board they took everyplace with them. They let Ira's hair grow long and it used to bounce up and down when he was dancing on his board. He was always real sweet to me and walked me to the store for gum or candy when I was little and took me wading in the creek and then he taught me how to clog, too, then I'd jump up and dance with him on his board sometimes and the crowd just went wild, everybody loved that.

So I remember my whole family together, very sweet times, mostly with the music, and then Daddy and Ira got killed on the way back from Knoxville, Tennessee, coming down the famous turn at Twin Peaks in a freak March snowstorm when Daddy's brakes failed. I was almost eleven when this happened, and I never did get to have my birthday party. I have played it over and over in my mind a thousand times, the crew-cut trooper at the door with his round hat in his hands, Mama's screams, how she fell down on the ground in the snow. Up until that point, my life had been mostly music and sunshine. And slow, real slow, like it was all happening under the bell jar in Old Rellar's parlor.

"DEE DEE? DEE Dee? Where are you, baby?" All of a sudden Willie is thrashing around in the bed like a crazy boy. Sometimes he does this.

"Here," I say. "Right here." And I go back in there and get back on the mattress and hold him in my arms and sing that song Mama used to sing to me when I was a little girl.

Hush little baby, don't you cry,
Go to sleep little baby
When you wake, you shall have
All the pretty little horses
Hush a bye, don't you cry
Go to sleep little baby
When you wake, you'll have a sweet cake
And all the pretty little horses.

Endangered

Dear Paula,

This is me Dee Dee writing to you again from the sunshine state thats what they call it, where things are not so sunny despite of all you have taught us and told us. I mean you got us out of the life but now we are in a nother life where things are not going too good ether. This letter is about Tamika.

The word for Tamika is *endangered*.

You remember when I told you about the nice man that gave us this cute little pink trailer with the round top? Well that is Tony Marchant, but he is not nice as I thought at first, he smiles all the time, which creeps me out and he is always up to something. The word for Tony is *duplicitous*. He says he owns this little trailer park with his brother but he does not appear to work at all and he has been coming around here a lot lately and yesterday when I came back from the Tree House him and Tamika was laying on the bed smoking cigarettes and looking at a science fiction movie on TV with the blinds shut, you could not tell if it was night or day in there and the trailer was filled with smoke. These ghosty-looking beings from Outer Space were making ghosty shapes on the wall all fluttery and weird.

It is a land beyond your wildest dreams, one of those big-headed sci-fi beings said.

Come on over here, Dee Dee, Tony Marchant said, patting the bed, which was all messed up, we have got lotsa room he said, and we'd love to have some company. He is a big, fat, greasy slob in my opinion. Tamika kept on giggling and my heart just sank for I knew she was high.

Aren't you supposed to be at work? I said, and Tamika said, Well I am home sick, cant you tell? And just fell out laughing as of old, that old bad Tamika that was so cute. You remember how we used to have such a good time.

You better get up from there and put on your uniform and go on over to the I Hop to work right this minute, I said, and she said Oh yeah Miss Good Girl? Is that right Miss Rich Girl? and she was real high so I left and walked over to the I Hop myself and got me a chicken biscuit and one to bring back for Tamika.

Tony was gone by then and she was laying in the bed all messed up crying and crying. Oh God, she said. She held out her arms.

I turned the sound down on the TV and went over

there and hugged her. You have got to not do this, I said. Remember what Paula said?

Oh Dee Dee you don't know nothing, she said. You in love. You gone all the time. You don't know what's happening now.

What, I said. What are you talking about?

I am talking about Jamal, she said and I said Oh yeah for you remember that is her baby boy that her auntie is keeping for her now up in Knoxville.

Well, Tamika said, the auntie called and said Jamal is real sick all of a sudden, he has got a blood disease and he has to have transfusions that cost a lot of money, and she wants me to send more money.

Oh Tamika, I say, I am so sorry. So I laid down on the bed beside her and hugged her. I love Tamika like a sister you know.

I have got to get some more money, Tamika said.

Well you better hold onto this job then, I said, rubbing her on the shoulder. Tamika has the prettiest skin, she is kind of a tan color, real pretty, she has this heart tattoo on her shoulder and a heart shaped face too. Her eyes are real big. She twisted around to look at me.

No I mean real money, Tamika said. Can you help me?

I will do what I can, I said, but my heart was going down and down. I got this real bad feeling in my gut.

Well me and Tony was thinking maybe you can look around over there where you're working for those rich people and see if they is got some pills just sitting in the medicine cabinets someplace. Tony says old people get a lot of prescriptions they're not using, they never even miss them. He say he can get a lot of money for pills.

And my heart sank even more because I got it then, what was going on with Tony.

Well I can look, I said, but I don't think they've got any pills or anything like that around over there.

This was a lie. There was a ton of pills in Miss Susan's little house and I knew right where they are, in the bottom dresser drawer in her bedroom and in the medicine cabinet in the bathroom. I bet there were some pills just laying around over there in the big house too, Mr. Atlas was so messy.

Just look and see, Tamika said real pitiful. Please, Dee Dee, and I said I would, and then laid down beside her and started singing Sweet Dreams which she always loved and she started singing with me too until finally she went to sleep breathing in and out, in and out like a little child, like her own little Jamal that she does not have. They took him away when she got sent up for drugs the third time, that's when she came into the Program. So I just laid there next to Tamika and hugged her and watched her breathing in and out while that ghosty sci-fi movie made flicker lights and random shapes and pictures on the wall and it was beautiful and safe in our own little pink trailer again though now I know it is not.

I was just thinking about the Program and how we used to make popcorn and watch movies all together on the TV and you showed us how to make banana pudding which was so good and I have never had one bite of since. And the time at that state park when we took the nature hike through the swamp on the raised up wooden walkway and saw the alligator and how Janeen tried to run away when we went to the toilets but did not get far, ha ha that trucker brought her back when he got in his cab and found her. I never thought I would say those were the good old days ha ha!

So here comes Lots of Love from Me Dee Dee!

Intervention

~~~~~~~~~~~~~~~~~~~~

The kids are coming for lunch today, not Herb's idea, so he knows something is up, and he definitely knows he's not gonna like it. His daughter Ashley and her smart-ass, candy-ass husband, Abe, the psychologist with the shit-eating grin, *just happen* to be coming down from Del Ray for a conference in Key West—conference, my ass!—and Marcie, his professor daughter from New York City, *just happens* to be in the Keys with some friends for spring break (*where?* he'd like to know, there's no place worth going in the Keys except for Key West) so she's *popping in*, too, so Maribeth thought it would just be so lovely to have a family lunch, so Pat organized the whole thing. And Herb has got to hand it to her, Pat can organize anything. Some outfit named A Moveable Feast is bringing the whole damn lunch, who knows what, and Maria is making her specialty, tres leches cake, Herb's favorite, for dessert. Herb doesn't have to do a damn thing but show up, Pat says. Well, what if he doesn't *want* to show up?

What if he wants to take a drive up the Keys in his Porsche Carrera instead? Just like he used to do with Susan, just driving with the top down and the wind in your face and that aqua-blue water stretching out flat on both sides of you and no particular destination in mind, maybe get a margarita and some of that great turtle soup at the Green Turtle Inn and then spend the night at the Beacon hotel up in Miami, South Beach, that's the ticket.

But the Porsche keys are not hanging on their hook in the laundry room anymore, that hook in the line of hooks where all the other keys are still hanging, that same hook the Porsche keys have been hanging on ever since he bought the car. Lucky thing he's got another set of Porsche keys that even Susan never knew about, stuck in the toe of one of those old two-tone golf shoes in his closet—now in his own pants pocket. Herb's not gonna say a word about any of that, but he fingers the keys as he sits in the sun and watches Renee—not her real name, he's sure of it now, there's always a beat before she reacts when anybody says it—fooling with Susan's new hairdo.

She fixed Susan's hair herself, this so-called Renee, she just announced she could and she *did*, she brought all the stuff and gave Susan a haircut one day and then a bleach job the next, Susan sitting absolutely still in the big puffy chair with her shoulders covered by towels and kind of smiling while Renee worked on her hair, singing the entire time. Joan Baez, Emmylou Harris, stuff Susan likes. When Herb told Renee she had a great voice, Renee said well you should hear my roommate Tamika! Now *she* can really sing! So who knew this

Renee has a roommate? And where do they live, this Renee and this Tamika? Every time Herb offers to take her home, Renee just laughs and runs off to get the bus except a coupla times when it's been raining, she lets him drive her over there someplace near Searstown and then she just jumps out and vanishes, throwing a thank you back over her shoulder.

Renee is maybe a little more dressed up than usual today, because of this family visit no doubt. She's got her shiny yellow hair up in this kind of bun thing like an old-maid schoolteacher instead of the usual, a kid with two pigtails or the ponytail, and she's got little shell earrings on along with her blue tunic and her white pants and tennis shoes.

Herb has this fantasy that he's had a lot of times that she's gonna just start singing "Let Me Entertain You" and strip it all off like a stripper, but of course that's nuts, he's batshit. Something else is gonna happen today, something very damn different. There's a word for what's gonna happen today— fuck, what is it? *Intervention.* Yeah, he's got this feeling. Yeah.

His Susan smiles at nobody, stretching her thin arms, while Renee fools with her hair, the new haircut like a little cap, what did Renee call it? "Kind of a pixie," and when Herb said what the hell is a pixie, she giggled and said, "You know, like Tinker Bell," who has the ability to just fly away, Herb knows, which his Susan can never, *ever* do again, she's stuck with this body, which is not her body, and this brain, which is not her brain, forever.

"Be right back," Herb says, and slowly gets up to pee. Damn hip hurts. Too far to go inside so he ducks behind the strangler fig tree, the biggest thing in Susan's little garden, and pees forever it seems, dribbles is more like it, finally coming back around the big gnarled trunk to see none other than Dr. Abe Beerman, his son-in-law, standing there grinning like the fool he is, big black moustache and beard, chinos and sandals and a loose white embroidered shirt that makes him look like a cross between a guru and a folk singer, very smart. *Guru to the geezers*, very effective down here in Florida, which is filled with geezers. Shit. Herb puts out his hand. "How are you, Doc?"

"How are *you*, Herb? I think that's more to the point." Dr. Abe does his two-handed trademark clasp for a beat too long, meant to be reassuring no doubt but a little too warm for Herb, who has never been into touching men. But women!— well, that's another story.

"Good to see you," Herb lies, finally getting his hand back, turning toward Renee standing by Susan in her chair in the little garden in the sun. *Exhibit A*, he's thinking. They've all gotta be impressed.

"Not so fast, sir." Dr. Abe points to Herb's fly, which Herb zips up with some effort. Hell, it's a long way down there, Mexico, South America, another country. Anything can happen down south.

He follows Dr. Abe across the grass to Susan's chair, where Ashley seems to be talking very seriously to Renee while Susan looks and looks at a big red hibiscus flower, which someone, probably Renee, has put into her hands. Still, she's happy, anybody can see that. And she looks good, too, wearing a white blouse and flowered slacks, very classy.

"Daddy!" Ashley turns to kiss him. She's red-haired and

freckled with big, wide, trusting gray eyes, the very picture of her mother, back in the day. Herb's first and best love, his sainted Roxana. His heart skips a beat but he's not telling. He hugs Ashley tight and she smells clean and fresh, like laundry. How'd she ever end up with this snake-oil jerk? That's the question.

"There you are!" Pat calls from the door of the big house with Maribeth right behind her, long blond hippie hair, long yellow hippie sundress and sandals, rings on her toes. "Come on, Maria has made flan and tres leches, and look who's here!" and whaddya know Herb's professor daughter Marcie comes running out to hug him, big tortoiseshell glasses, khaki pantsuit, she'll never get another husband, but what the fuck. Who needs one? Who needs a man anyhow?

"Shall I go get Mama? Or help bring her in?" Marcie asks, but both Pat and Maribeth shake their heads *no*, firmly, Maribeth's fine blond hair flying out and then settling back on her shoulders.

"Too many people, too confusing," Pat says in a tone that means business. "Renee will walk Susan out to her own little house, Maria has already taken their lunch over there for them. Then hopefully Susan won't get so agitated."

"Renee appears to be quite the godsend," Marcie remarks, and Herb catches the way Ashley and Dr. Abe look at each other, like they've got a secret or something. *What the fuck?* But the lunch from A Moveable Feast is damn good even if cooked by weirdos, what the hell, and Maria has outdone herself on the desserts, all of it served on Susan's Italian pottery, and even Susan herself would have approved of Maribeth's fancy table setting with those orchids blooming in the center of the big round marble table. Susan would have loved it all, she loved everything elegant. Herb can't eat much, though— he's got killer indigestion, even though he took his Prilosec, or he's pretty sure he took it. He wishes he was out there in the little house with his own crazy Susan and not-Renee, what the hell. He wouldn't even mind a little rat-a-tat-tat.

Everybody around the beautiful table is very cheerful, too cheerful. Ashley announces that the twins have both been accepted to the colleges of their choice, early admission, Brown and Wooster, "That's in Ohio, Daddy, an excellent school, too, though you may not have heard of it."

What's the matter with Florida? Herb's thinking. So they're too good for Florida, these famous grandsons of his?

Marcie approves the choices, then mentions that actually she has some news, too, she has just been named Associate Professor and head of the comparative literature department at Hunter College, with tenure, of course.

"Literature as compared to what?" Herb asks, and Marcie smiles. "Other literature, I guess, Daddy," getting a laugh.

"And what's tenure?" Herb asks.

"Tenure means they can't fire me," she tells him.

"Yeah? No matter what you do?"

"That's right, Daddy," Marcie says, and Herb nods. Good for her. Now there's a deal.

Herb has never heard of such a thing but it doesn't sur- prise him because Marcie was always the hard worker, the good one, the Girl Scout, the president of the class, on and on. Marcie got all that goodness from her mother, who never lived to see her grow up. But his Roxana loved fun, too, teasing, laughing, singing, dancing the night away. Marcie always looks like she's in a meeting.

So does Dr. Big Deal, who clears his throat and leans forward now, looking carefully, professionally, from face to face around the festive table, letting the silence build, making eye contact with everybody, making sure he's got their full attention. This is a *technique*, Herb's sure of it. Shit! He feels like screaming. *Go ahead! What the fuck? Just say it!* But he doesn't.

His pretty Ashley leans forward, too. She's like the slave of this guy.

Pat reaches out to take Maribeth's hand.

Damn. Something heavy is coming down all right.

"In every long life," Dr. Big Deal announces, in this deep, fakey voice, like the voice of God or James Earl Jones or somebody, "the time arrives. The time—the *opportunity*— for change, for growth, for moving forward into an easier, more pleasant, more fruitful and manageable life. This time has arrived for you, Herb. You have earned this. You and your beautiful, beloved Susan. You have taken absolutely wonderful care of her throughout her devastating illness. You are taking wonderful care of her now. We all regret that this ideal situation, which you have created here, cannot continue indefinitely, Herb—"

"Oh yeah? Is that so? And why the hell not, Abe?" Herb hits the table with both hands, but Abe continues calmly on without even missing a beat.

"—due to your own failing health." Dr. Wonderful looks

around the table again, from face to face, to emphasize these words. "But as luck would have it, your daughter Ashley and I are in a position to address this crisis and help you solve the problem. As luck would have it, I have recently been named director and head physician of a marvelous new state-of-the-art facility, the Atrium at Del Ray Beach, offering continual and loving residential care at all levels. In fact, Ashley and I have already made a down payment on one of the most luxurious homes at the Atrium in order to secure it for you. And most importantly, the Arbor, a special unit for advanced Alzheimer's patients, is directly across the beautiful little canal outside your own front door. A stone's throw away. So you will see your beloved Susan every day, as often as you wish to see her, but you will never have to worry about her care again as you deal with your own serious health issues."

Herb slams the table so hard that the crystal jumps. "You can't do this, Bucko," he says flatly.

"No Herb, my friend, *you* can't do this," Dr. Abe intones in that deep, serious, but loving voice of God, which Herb hates.

But nobody else says a word. Herb looks from person to person around the table. Ashley is white-faced, biting her lip resolutely as she clasps her husband's hand. Maribeth starts to cry quietly now, clinging to solemn Pat. Marcie looks collected and resigned, much older, infinitely sad. *They know*, Herb realizes suddenly. What the fuck? This is a setup. They know. They came here knowing. They all know his diagnosis. Herb can't even imagine how. Some fancy doctor deal, no doubt. All these hotshot docs are crooks.

Then Pat clears her throat and stands up. She walks around the table to put her hands on Herb's shoulders and squeeze, the first time she has ever touched him like this. "Hey buddy," she says, "they all love you, you old goat, got it? They all love you, and they love Susan, and they wanna help. That's all. Now, let's all go into the solarium for coffee."

"What is this? What coffee? What the fuck? You running a three-star hotel in here today?" Herb manages to say, which makes everybody laugh for some reason, and then Ashley and Marcie each grab an arm and suddenly Herb is being escorted in style past the Chihuly glass sculpture and through the big arched doors into the solarium where SURPRISE! It's exactly like that old game show, "This is your life, Herbert Atlas!" Everybody's there.

Gloria sits on the white sofa in a red suit and red high heels. She looks like a million dollars. "Hi honey," she says, giving him that big old smile.

His nephew Marco jumps up, porkpie hat in hand, spitting image of Herb's brother Donnie, and rushes forward to hug him, crying big man-sobs, and the jig is totally up. Only T-Boy is not here, thank God. Well, somebody's got to run the company.

"We are going to a hukilau, where the mau-mau meets the chow-chow—" and it's David, Susan's lawyer son from Raleigh, with his very blond, very Southern country-club wife Mary Page, both of them all dressed up like they're going to a funeral, for Christ's sake. Which, in a way, they are. "Herbert, you did great! You've done great, man! Now you need to take care of yourself." David bursts into tears as he hugs Herb. His wife trots around handing out pink Kleenex from her purse.

"Sit down, sit down," Pat says. "Maria?"

Maria brings in more coffee and some kind of little rolled-up cookies. *Shit*. Herb feels like he's in a play.

He sits down on the sofa next to Gloria, who takes his hand. "Honey, I'm so sorry," she says.

Ricky slips in to stand near the door, inscrutable with his hat pulled low over his face, wearing shades and a white linen jacket. He does not sit down for this entire conference or meeting or whatever the hell it is, which Herb understands and appreciates.

Dr. Wonderful takes over, warm and smiling. "Just so we're all on the same page," he begins. He reads an email from Brian, Herb's gay son in Manhattan, who says that Brian is in favor of whatever his sister and Dr. Beerman feel is best for Herb. Brian says he loves his father. He says he also loves somebody named David Allan Lockhart, and he would like to take this opportunity to announce that they have agreed to marry.

"Oh, isn't that sweet?" Mary Page sings out, "Every cloud has a silver lining!" which cracks everybody up. Maria passes the cookies around again, some kind of almond flavor. They are delicious.

"Now as I was saying," Dr. Abe begins again, settling them all down, "Herbert has not been well for some time." He pauses, looking at Herb. "Do you want me to do this, Herb? Or do you want to tell them yourself?"

"I got nothing to tell," Herb says. "What I want is, I want

you to shut up and get your ass back to Del Ray as soon as possible. ASAP. This party's over. Glad you could make it."

"Now Daddy!" Ashley cries out.

This is when Ricky suddenly slides forward. He's not there and then he is there, taking over. He removes his shades and puts them in his breast pocket, then touches the brim of his hat, inclining his head. "Ricky Estevez," he says, "Stepson and lifelong pal of Mr. Herbert Atlas, a prince. Do not forget that. A prince. I'm sorry for telling everyone, Herb, but at some point, your family needs to know, and you have to face the music. So yeah, I can give you all the goods here, short and sweet. Mr. Atlas has been sick for a long time. A very long time, it appears. It may be that he went to a physician years ago, in Jacksonville. It may be that he received some advice at that point, which he did not follow." Gloria nods. "In any case, by the time Mr. Atlas consulted the doctor here in Key West several weeks ago, the situation had become acute. The diagnosis is stage-four prostate cancer with bone metastases, the cancer showing up now all along his spine, ribs, and clavicle. They've started him on hormone therapy, which may be able to stop the growth of the bone metastases, maybe even shrink some of the lesions, but eventually that will stop working. Mr. Atlas's prognosis—" Ricky pauses, looking all around at everyone in the solarium—"is not good." Ricky crosses over to the couch to throw an arm around Herb's neck, hugging him from behind. "So sorry, man. I love you."

Gloria brings Herb's hand up to her lips and kisses it as the room bursts into a hubbub, quelled by Dr. Abe.

"There you have it." He spreads his arms wide. "Thank you, Richard."

"It's just Ricky." Ricky tips his hat to the doctor.

Dr. Big clears his throat. "There you have it," he begins again. "Herbert needs treatment. Susan needs professional continuing care. Their lovely new home in the Atrium awaits."

"Fuck the Atrium," Herb says.

Ricky grins. "Maybe a little more time, mon?" he says.

"Susan needs continuing care from a *licensed caregiver*," Dr. Abe continues. "A geriatric specialist."

"Listen, I'm telling you, we're doing okay here," Herb says. "Between Renee and the Home Health girls, we're doing just fine. Susan loves Renee, you might have noticed. Renee has changed everything around here."

Ashley clears her throat. "Daddy, Renee is *not* a licensed caregiver."

"So who said she was? She's a—whaddya call it? She's a manicure girl, a pedicure girl, a very nice girl. She never said she was a nurse. Nobody ever said she was a nurse. The point is, Susan loves her. I'm not kidding. She can do miracles with Susan."

Ashley and Dr. Abe look at each other intensely, significantly, across the couch.

"Herbert," Dr. Abe intones, "We have been checking—or trying to check—on Renee. The fact is that she is simply not registered anyplace, for anything. She is not even a registered nail technician, much less a caregiver of any sort."

Pat speaks up. "In fact, we suspect that Renee may be

some sort of a gold-digger, a 'nurse with a purse,' as the saying goes. Renee may even be an assumed name."

Herb explodes. "Who cares what her name is? She does nails! She does hair! She sings like a pro! She's just a girl—a sweet girl, a nice girl—and she's better with Susan than I am, or any one of you—she's a damn genius with Susan. So, thanks but no thanks. We're doing okay here. We're doing just fine."

"Of course it will take some time to get used to all these new ideas and changes." Dr. Nice has a new soothing voice. "Now we've got just a few preliminary forms for you to sign . . ."

"Forms, my ass!" Herb stands up with effort, and Gloria's help.

Ricky takes Dr. Abe's arm in a classy gesture, showing him smoothly toward the front door.

"Hey! Hey!" Dr. Abe cries out just as the doorbell rings, its Hawaiian melody rippling through the house.

"I get it." Maria opens the door to admit Renee, blond as an angel with a big smile on her face.

"Goodbye everybody," she says. "Lisa, the next Home Health lady, is already here, she's in there with Miss Susan now, I put a Western movie on for them, so I'll be leaving. I just wanted to tell you all how nice it was to meet Miss Susan's whole family." Standing in her patch of sunlight, Renee smiles sweetly at them all, then shuts the door.

Buffalo

~~~~~~

Fuck! Who the hell invited all those people, that's what Herb would like to know. And then where did they all go? Now Herb sits alone in a lawn chair in Susan's little garden, Susan asleep inside with the goddamn Home Health girl watching over her, Susan asleep for once, to dream whatever dreams are possible these days, who knows what goes on in that blond pixie head? Herb feels himself slipping back, back, back through time to the days when it was only himself and Roxana, just children for Christ's sake, back in the old neighborhood in Buffalo—Parkside, next to the zoo and Delaware Park. He was, what?, ten, eleven years old when he met her, and her one year younger, with a big green bow in the middle of all her long, red curls, those knobby knees, the big green kneesocks and the saddle shoes, the green plaid skirt, her school uniform. Now that was one cute outfit. Herb can see her right now as she was then, a doll. Just a doll, in memory as in life, that funny, big, lopsided grin, she was always ready to have fun, Roxana. Game for anything. She was crying though, that day he met her in Delaware Park. She had wrecked her bike and hurt her knee—red blood! above the green wool sock—when Herbert came riding along on his bike whistling, not a care in the world, who knew this scrawny little redheaded girl would put a stamp on the rest of his life forever?

He got off his bike and pulled her up by her skinny white arms and she sat there smiling at him through her tears and talking a mile a minute while he fixed her bicycle chain, which took maybe all of five minutes. Nothing to it! The big hero, he held her bike steady while she got on and then he followed her wobbling home to the flat where she lived with her mother and brothers and sister, where everybody had to keep quiet whenever Mr. Duffy, a night watchman at Civic Stadium, was asleep. That first day, Roxana's mother gave him and Roxana some soda bread still warm from the oven while her little red-headed brothers and one sister gathered around him, pushing and shoving, like he was a show in the circus.

"He saved my life!" Roxana declared, real dramatic. Oh yeah, she was a drama queen, all right. She could have gone on the stage and in fact she was in every one of those damn holy dramas they used to put on over there at her fucked-up Catholic School, nun of this and nun of that in Herb's opinion, but who was he to say, some little Jew boy. Roxana had a great singing voice, too.

Her mother's kitchen was big and rowdy with potted plants on the windowsills and sun coming in the windows and bubbling pots on the stove and everybody talking at once, pretty different from Herb's home where he and his older brother Al lived with his mother and his grandmother in a dark, narrow third-floor walk-up where all they ever ate was cabbage and all they ever heard about was how bad things were and where was the next meal coming from. Down on men, too, both of them, no wonder Al and then Herb got out of there as soon as they could.

But Roxana's mother was cheery and nice, and Roxana herself was a ray of sunshine. When Herb finally left her flat that first day, he was trying to think of something to say, some way to see her again, but he got tongue-tied all of a sudden out there on the stoop and then she just piped up (easy, easy, everything was easy for Roxana), "Hey you wanna ride bikes in the park next Saturday morning?" and Herb said yes and that was that. Signed, sealed, and delivered, his whole life, before he even turned twelve.

She went to Holy Angels Catholic girls school and he went to P.S. 54 on Main Street, but they owned the city in those days, riding their bikes. They were the best friends in the world. All those *adventures*, she always called them, like they were kids in a book, for Christ's sake. In between his jobs (delivering groceries for Old Man Hogg, running errands for the widow sisters, sweeping off the stoops and the sidewalk for the super), they found time to ride to Parkside Candy, between Parkside and Hertel, where he spent his wages on penny candy or an ice-cream cone for a nickel. You couldn't ride with a cone in your hand, though. You had to park and sit on the curb to eat it. They rode those bikes everyplace. In summer, they rode under the viaduct. Bikes tossed aside, they played Truth or Dare or told stories while the traffic roared above them and sometimes gravel dropped in the grass beside them. Roxana loved to make up stories, she got him into it.

Later they rode the trolley, too—for ten cents, they could go all over Buffalo. They saw Santa in Finkel's at Christmastime and real live Eskimos in an exhibit at the museum. They saw Warren Spahn pitch at an exhibition game in Offermann Stadium thanks to Roxana's daddy who took them all, all the kids. Warren Spahn had grown up in the neighborhood.

Herb's own father had killed himself in the Depression, hanged himself in the coat closet just inside the apartment door. Herb could barely remember him. A thin man with black glasses, stooped over. Herb loved Roxana's daddy, who loved the demon rum, however. Sometimes the kids would be tiptoeing all around him still dressed in his watch-man uniform passed out drunk on the davenport or in the middle of the floor, where he'd then sleep all day. There was always something going on at Roxana's, which was not true at Herb's. He was drawn to all of them, the Duffys, but especially to *her*, Roxana, like a moth to a flame. They took him in like an orphan.

In wintertime they all went sledding in Delaware Park and Roxana and her sister laughed and laughed about the statue of David with his fig leaf. By then, at twelve or thirteen, Herb already knew he was going to marry her even though his brother gave him unending shit about it all the time. Al was gone a lot by then, running the numbers for Big Eddy Kaminski, and then he dropped out of school and got in trou-ble and then he went in the army, which was the making of

him, everybody said. Their mother put all of Al's stuff in a
cardboard box and rented out his room to a big mean lady
named Mrs. Brickenmeyer who ran the lingerie department at
Nolen's, and then later, when Herb graduated high school and
went in the army, too, she rented out his room, as well. His
grandmother died and his mother didn't even write and tell
him. After that Herb didn't have a home anymore. It was like
they had never lived there, like they had never been a family
at all. Roxana's family, that was Herb's family by then. So
whaddya think, it's weird to marry your sister? But it wasn't
like that at all.

Stolen Drugs

It was raining cats and dogs—that's what grandma used to say up home—when I got on the bus with the drugs, I swear I was so nervous riding along with all those little bottles in that big plastic Rite Aid bag. They were in another bag inside it, also Rite Aid but smaller, all taped up, plus some other stuff from Rite Aid such as a cheap purple hippie dress and a beach towel with a shark on it and a four-pack of toilet paper, just in case anybody thought to look in there. I was sweating like crazy on that bus, even in the rain.

I had not ever stole from a client before, though Tamika was right, Mr. Atlas's room was so messy—I mean the whole Master Wing, that's what they called it—was so messy that nobody would ever miss a thing. There were pills for both him and Miss Susan just left in the medicine cabinet or throwed into a couple old shoeboxes that Mr. Atlas had in the back of his great big closet, the Master Closet is what they called it. I took a lot but I left some, too, and I was fixing to hightail it out of that creepy big suite with its king-size blue satin bed when I thought to look in *her* closet, or what used to be her closet before they moved her down to her little house, and it made me so sad to see all her jackets and pantsuits and beautiful dresses just hanging there on the hangers like a whole army of Miss Susans that would never walk again nor see the light of day. A row of shelves to the side was filled with her old pocketbooks and designer bags and fancy little purses and all of a sudden I thought to look in one of those, too, Kate Spade I think it was, and Bingo I found a *motherlode* (word) in that one, Vicodin and Oxycodone and Percocet and Lortab and I don't know what all, so I went through some more purses, too, but then I got spooked, all of a sudden I felt like somebody was watching me, seeing what all I had done, even though I knew Mr. Atlas was at the doctor up in Marathon for some tests, and Maria had gone shopping at the big Publix out on Route 1. But I just felt strange all of a sudden like I was on drugs myself, which I will never be again. I swear this on the soul of my little sister Ida Rose that died.

So I skedaddled out of there and stopped to buy things at Rite Aid and caught the bus and headed back out to our trailer with my teeth just chattering up a storm, like I was cold though I was not. The sun was starting to come out when I got off the bus at Roosevelt, but I had to step across a fallen branch and walk through a lot of puddles on the way. Some of the puddles had oil in them, which made them real pretty and shiny, *iridescent* is the word for that, but I myself was feeling real guilty and confused. *Traitorous* is the word for me. I ducked through the bushes and I was there.

The sweet old Black lady in number 4, Miss Violet, was sitting out in front of her silver Airstream smoking a cigarette and hollered at me, did I want some banana bread, she had just made some, but I shook my head no even though all of a sudden I was just starving. I knew I didn't deserve any banana bread. But then I thought, wait! I have got to take care of my little baby now, that's the main thing I've got to do, so I went back and got two pieces from her and gobbled them right up.

This was a good thing because our own trailer didn't have any food at all, not a thing, when I got the key out from under the cinder block and let myself in.

"Tamika?" I called.

Nobody home. It was a real mess in there, bed not made and pizza boxes all over and the sink full of dirty dishes. Clothes and trash covered the floor, Tamika's and his both, including some rolling papers and one empty prescription pill bottle, which made my heart sink.

I had just finished washing the dishes when Tamika came in and squealed and gave me a big kiss and a hug. Then she held me out at arm's length to look at me good. "Did you get any?" she asked. Her hair was real big and she looked good, sort of sparky. But I could smell it on her, a smell I knew down in my bones.

"You're doing it, aren't you? All of it," I could not keep from saying.

She slapped me across the face. "You don't know nothing. That don't matter. Nothing matters but my baby, Jamal. He's so sick and he's got to get these treatments. You don't have a baby so you don't know nothing about it."

"Well, I am going to have a baby, too, I am, Tamika!" My face hurt. "My own little baby just like you got. And I am going to have a husband, too."

"Wait a minute. You shittin' me?" Tamika grabbed ahold of my shoulders. "You're gonna have a baby with that rich boy?"

I was smiling and crying at the same time. All I could do was nod. Then I put my arms out and she hugged me tight, I do love Tamika, she is my other me. "And I got something for you, too," I said. "Something for Jamal."

I pulled the plastic bag out from under the bed. "There's a lot in there," I said. "That's gonna be a lot of money, may be enough for you to get out of here."

"No, I got the doctor report and he's so sick, I ain't gonna get out of here anytime soon, honey," Tamika said. "But it don't matter, don't nothing matter now but Jamal."

"Oh, that's not true, Tamika. You matter. Don't you remember what Paula said?"

"Paula is gone."

"Well, you're not gone. Listen, let's go to Disney World. Don't you remember how we said we've got to go to Disney World and see the Princesses? Well, we could still go." This was always our dream.

"You ain't going no place, honey, not if you're pregnant. Don't you know nothing? But you know Tony can fix that."

"No," I said. "I am going to get married," I said. "Me and him we love each other."

"Does he even know you're pregnant?"

"Of course he does," I said, but I was never much good at lying, that is one of my problems.

"Of course he don't," Tamika said, hugging me. "But don't you worry, honey." For a minute she looked like her old sweet self, her girl self, when we were in the program together. "Tony can fix anything. Anything. You're going to be all right. But you don't need no baby."

Tony came in the door right then, a lot smaller and more weaselly than I remembered him being. He kept his black hair slicked back just so, and he had that nasty black moustache that went down the sides of his mouth and looked awful, and little black eyes that jumped around, jumped around. He liked to act like he was one of the Sopranos. Tony does not miss a trick.

"Well if it ain't the Princess come down here to see us poor folks," he said, grinning a big, wide nasty grin. "What brings you down in this part of the world, girl? You slumming?"

I picked up the plastic Rite Aid bag and handed it to him. "This is not for you," I said. "This is for Tamika."

"Nice," Tony said. "You come back anytime, hon, you hear me? And bring us another little something."

"I will," I said.

"You got a beer, baby?" Tony said to Tamika, so she got him one and a Fireball for herself.

"You sure you don't want one of these, Dee Dee?" Tamika asked me. "They fix you up real good."

But I shook my head no and grabbed some more of my clothes to take back to the Tree House. I knew I couldn't stay here no more. Any more. Any longer. I cannot stay here any longer, this is my *resolution* (word). It is not safe, for me or my baby. It is *hazardous* (word). I hugged Tamika extra hard before I left, pushing three twenty-dollar bills down in her jeans pocket right before I went out the door.

"You be good now," I called back, and Tamika said, "Yeah, right," sounding sad, different.

I almost ran down the road.

"Come sit with me a minute, Dee Dee," Miss Violet called from her chair in front of her Airstream. "I've got some more of that banana bread."

"No ma'am," I said, "I've got to go on home now. Thanks so much though."

The sun was coming out again finally, just in time for sunset. I looked back at the little trailer park right before I ducked through the bushes and left—four beat-up trailers and five campers on a muddy road, three of the campers empty. The old couple in the green trailer, No. 8, were sitting out to get some fresh air, too. It's always real fresh after it rains. They waved at me and I waved back. Our pink trailer was cute all right, it looked like a toy sitting up on the rise at the end of the row on two wheels and two cinder blocks. It ain't going no where. But I am, I said to myself. I am, me Dee Dee.

Failure to Thrive

Dee Dee can't even remember that time after her daddy and Ira died unless she goes way, way up in her head above it all, above their log house by the side of the road and the mountains all around them, old kind mountains she always thought. And she had loved that little house.

But Mama did not act like herself anymore. And there was a long time Dee Dee doesn't remember very good at all, a lot of people in and out of the house, staying sometimes for a day or two, before they finally lost the house, that's how her mama put it, "We lost the house," and then she took Dee Dee and moved back up into the real mountains of Madison County, where her mama got a job in their cousin's convenience store, jerking Dee Dee out of school right before the play she was in, *Annie Get Your Gun*, where she had had the part of Annie.

Dee Dee didn't much like her new school up there, they didn't have music or art, and she didn't like her mama's new friends so much either, especially this one man that kept coming around more and more, Smiley Dollar, from over in Tennessee he said. He used to play music with some of Mama's kin but he was not from around there.

Smiley Dollar was a big, slow-moving, fast-talking man with a smile that never left his face, Dee Dee knows the word now, it is *insinuating*. Smiley Dollar always looked like he had a secret or like he knew more than you knew, even more than you knew about you. He liked to touch people when he talked to them, too, but Dee Dee hated that, and pulled away.

"It's all right, Little Sister," he'd say. "You're gonna come around."

Not hardly, Dee Dee was thinking, even then, at eleven.

But he did make Mama feel a lot better with the pills he gave her, she calmed down pretty good and got kind of dreamy, which was good Dee Dee guessed but she hated it, too, sitting up in her favorite apple tree behind the house, cutting Daddy's initials into the bark with Ira's knife. The house was full of people coming and going all the time, mostly men, some of them sitting out on the porch picking with Smiley and trying to get Lacy to sing whenever they saw her, others just driving up the hill to park and run in and out. Money was changing hands.

Dee Dee washed her own clothes and did her homework and walked down the holler every morning to catch the bus to school where she kept her mouth shut and made *A*s, but then Smiley got busted and Mama got pregnant and when Smiley got out of jail they all moved over to Kettle Creek real fast in the dead of night, where they didn't know anybody or have any family. This was when Mama had Ida Rose, Dee Dee's tiny sister. Ida Rose was just as pretty as a doll and Dee Dee loved her to pieces, which was a good thing because Mama got real sick then and Dee Dee had to take care of them both while Smiley came and went and got his business going again. But Ida Rose was real little, too little, and she cried all the time, which made Smiley nervous because he had trouble sleeping anyway due to his PTSD, this is why one day he put Ida Rose out in the woodshed in February just for a little while so he could get a couple hours of peace and quiet.

Mama found her later and started screaming. Smiley blamed Dee Dee, saying he told her to bring Ida Rose back in when she quit crying, but he did not. Or Dee Dee was sure he did not, but then after awhile she was not sure of anything, and anyway Ida Rose died two days later. Froze to death, Dee Dee believed, though the home health nurse wrote "Failure to thrive" on the piece of paper. Dee thought it was her own fault that Ida Rose had frozen, and that's when she stopped caring what happened to herself anymore.

She kept going to school, but now she was sure people were talking about her, and she couldn't concentrate and her grades went down, and then her mother died, too, just slipped away. Buried in a little mountain cemetery in Tennessee with Ida Rose and no stone, though Smiley swore they were going to get one. After that it's not clear to Dee Dee what happened for a long time because Smiley was helping her out by then, giving her some pills to make her feel better and they did, and he slept with her to keep her warm so she would not freeze, too. Smiley had a mole on his back as big as a quarter and a tattoo of a lion on one arm and an eagle on the other and the name DEBI on the inside of his arm. One time Dee Dee said she wanted a tattoo but Smiley said he would never let her get one, he said she was too pretty. Sometimes he did things to her at night or made her do things to him and Dee Dee learned real fast that he was so big and strong it was no point in trying not to, so this is when she learned how to go up in her head, way up above that bed and that little house in Cooke County and even Tennessee, the whole state of Tennessee. Nobody can do anything to you if you're just not there.

She remembers when some church ladies came to the house bringing food (meat loaf! chocolate cake!) and clothes for her, and Smiley took the things at the door and did not ask them in, and then the next time the ladies came, he ran them off. Then the welfare lady came and took her away to the orphan school, which she hated because everybody was mean and made you pray all the time and spanked the kids with a ruler. So Dee Dee went of her own accord when Smiley showed up in a nice suit to get her out and take her to a new house where things would be different he said, though they were not. He had hooked up with a couple of guys and pretty soon he was in business again, cars coming up the holler at all times of the day and night.

Dee Dee never went back to school.

After he started doing pretty good, Smiley bought a new used Chevy Impala and drove Dee Dee to the mall in Waynesville where he bought her some cute clothes and got her a haircut and manicure and pedicure at the Beauty Box in the middle of the mall, leaving her there while he disappeared to talk to a man about something. Dee Dee loved it at the Beauty Box. She loved the gentle caressing touch of the manicure girl and the perfumey smells and the music in the background all the time. It was a different, sweeter world.

So this was Dee Dee's first mani-pedi and this is when she fell in love with nails forever and decided that's what she wanted to do, right then and there, at the Hilltopper Mall in Waynesville, N. C., and then Smiley came back and got her and took her out for supper at the Olive Garden where she had a chocolate milkshake and lasagna and then they went to a movie at the giant MoviePlex right there in the mall where the seats were as comfortable as armchairs and you could lean way back.

"Now how'd you like that?" Smiley said to her and she said she loved it and she thought Scarlett Johansson was so pretty. "Well, you're a helluva lot prettier than she is, honey," Smiley said, putting his hand on her knee. "You might be a movie star yourself," and when Dee Dee giggled, he said, "No, I'm telling you something here. You listen to me." But then he made her lean down and do something bad to him on the way home, he always got a kick out of doing it in a weird place like that, and then when they got back to the house Dee Dee went out back and threw up.

But she liked the pills by then, the way she didn't have to be there when she was there, and not long after that when Smiley said, "Honey, I need you to help me with the business now, why don't you have some fun with Steve here? Y'all have a good time now," pushing a skinny young truck driver toward her, Dee Dee heard herself saying "Well hey Steve, how you doing? Wanna hear some music?" And took him out to the screen porch in the back where Smiley had put a cot with an Indian blanket on it and Dee Dee's new transistor radio sat on the little table and she showed Steve that good time. She was good at it, even then. She didn't care, is the thing of it. She just didn't care. She didn't care about anything at all.

In the Garden

~~~~~~~~~~~~~~~~

Well, fuck! Herb thinks, coming out into Susan's garden. Look at this. He turns halfway back, putting up a hand to silence Ricky who drove him to Marathon for the MRI, what a crock that was. So who cares what's going on in there anyway? Who wants to know? "Que sera sera," that was a song he used to dance to, swinging the girls around, he used to be quite the dancer, light on his feet they all said. Who wants to know? Not Herb, for one. Who else wants to know? Not his son David, who doesn't give a damn, planning the wedding with his lover boy. Not Ricky. Not Marco, not Gloria. Who wants to know is Dr. Wonderful and Mrs. Wonderful, that's who. Plus Mrs. Dyke and Mrs. Dyke, that's who. What a crock.

And meanwhile, look at this!

Here's Susan, outside under the strangler fig, that enormous tree she's always loved so much, its huge, curling roots like sculpture behind the chair where she sits in the changing light and shade, wearing a big sparkly hat. Here's Susan sitting in front of a damn easel, so where'd she get the easel? Where'd she get the hat? Here's his Susan out in the dappled shade of the tree, big hat, head cocked, arm raised, shit! She's drawing at the easel! Like she's a damn artist or something. Herb turns his head, puts a finger up to his lips, sssh, to Ricky right behind him, who tips the brim of his hat, inclines his head in a nod. Got it.

And not-Renee is right there beside his Susan, of course, in another chair, saying something in Susan's ear . . . what? What the hell is she saying? Do they actually talk? Herb wonders. Not-Renee is like a—what is it?—horse whisperer or something. Like a crazy whisperer. Now she's laughing, and now Susan rips off a big sheet of paper from the easel and lets it flutter to the grass, pink swirly lines all over it. Crazy art. But here she is out in her garden, her own beloved garden, drawing for Christ's sake. Or painting. Whatever the fuck she's doing.

> PINK is the color of
> girls
> Valentines
> babies
> Key West
> bougainvillea
> clouds at sunset
> the girl I was

Not-Renee sees Herb, waves. "Come look, come look," she says, waving to them both. She pulls another big sheet of paper off this tablet she's got and stands to fasten it on the top of the easel, handing Susan another—what is it?—marker. A colored marker like kids use. Magic markers they used to call them. A red one this time. And Susan's just like a kid. She leans forward and starts right in, marking on the paper.

"Come see." Not-Renee stands up, gesturing for Herb to take her chair, which he does. Has to, in fact. Has to sit down. Ricky comes over bringing two more chairs from the round table in the gazebo. One for not-Renee, one for himself, which he places back at a little distance from the three of them. Ricky's always hanging back, watching silently, but he doesn't miss a thing.

"So where'd you get the easel?" Herb asks.

Not-Renee laughs, hand to her mouth. "Wal-Mart," she says. "Children's section."

"Pay for it yourself?"

She nods. Actually this is not true. The trailer park guy, Tony, took her in his van to get it, and he paid for it, along with some other stuff she and Tamika needed. Shampoo and milk and stuff. She shouldn't have let him pay for it but she didn't have enough money right then. Tony can act real nice when he wants to.

Herb shakes his head. "You coulda told me," he said. "I've got some money," at which she laughs out loud. He likes this girl. And look at Susan there, she's going to town with the damn red marker, now up and down, up and down all over the piece of paper, crazy stuff, she's sort of biting her tongue, but she's really into it, Herb sees.

> RED is the color of
> stoplights
> coleus
> thousands of tulips along the flat canal
> blood
> hearts beating and beating
> Valentines
> lipstick
> mani-pedi
> spaghetti

Not-Renee keeps smiling. She looks really pretty today, happy. Herb is hit by a sudden impulse.

"So what's going on with you lately, hon?" he asks her. "You doing okay? You happy? You like your job here?" Which will be all over soon, this job, bye-bye birdie, when the junta has their way. If they do.

Not-Renee smiles, a beautiful smile, hand up. "Yes sir. I'm real happy. I like it here."

Herb nods, both glad and sorry to hear this. It's getting pretty fucking complicated. A silence falls on them all, on the girl, on Susan making long, swirly strokes with her new red marker, on Ricky lounging way back in his chair with his hands in a little tent, watching them all.

Then the girl speaks into the silence, unexpectedly. "I'm

also real happy because I'm going to have a baby," she says with a big smile.

"Yeah? What the hell?" Herb sits up as best he can. "You married, honey?" He sure hasn't noticed any ring.

"Not yet." The girl picks up Susan's marker, which she has dropped, and hands it back to her, still smiling at Herb. "But we're going to get married real soon, we just haven't decided when yet. We haven't picked the date, but we are engaged."

"You sure about this? He knows about this baby?"

"Sure. We are betrothed." She is loving, no, *relishing* every word.

Dee Dee knows it's not true, but it feels like it's true, just as if she has made it true by saying the words, by putting them out in the sweet, warm air of this beautiful garden, Susan's garden, where they float in the scented breeze. Words have power, she knows this. She loves words, she loves Susan, and she loves this job. But she loves William the most of all. She adores William, she cherishes William, she is *infatuated* (word) and *enraptured* (word) by William, her intended, her *fiancé*, a word that she does not have a clue how to say out loud. But who cares? They are getting married! Forgetting to put her hand up, she smiles at them both, her snaggletoothed smile as bright as the sun.

Something for Dee Dee

Today I got to leave Miss Susan's house a little bit early because her daughter Ashley and that fancy doctor husband of hers came down from Del Ray for a little surprise visit, "popped in" is what they said. I wish I liked them better but I don't. I don't like the way they talk to me or the way he pulls on his fancy little beard. I don't like the way he looks at me, either, a way I have seen before. I bet he goes out on her. You can always tell.

I kissed Miss Susan goodbye on her white-white cheek but she didn't even notice, she was so busy drawing on her easel, she just loves it, I swear this is the best idea I have ever had.

"Bob! Would you just look at this! Pull that other chair over here and watch Mama, she actually seems to be concentrating! Who got her this easel, you?" Ashley twisted around to look at me.

I could feel myself blushing when I nodded. "Yes ma'am,"

I said, proud of it, but all she said was, "Fascinating. Bob, what do you make of this?"

But the doctor didn't say a thing, just sat down and leaned forward so I could see that he's got hair implants, which is not a surprise, I can always spot implants ever since beauty school. It looks like a row of little postholes got drilled in their head with a pinch of hair stuck down in each one. Dr. Abe had black-and-white hair both, pepper and salt they call it, very classy, very expensive.

I was ready to go but I needed to tell them some things since they'd be there alone with Miss Susan until the next Home Health lady, Sherry, came in about an hour. "Miss Susan just does one color at a time," I said, "so when her paper gets pretty full, you'll need to take that pad and pull off a new piece and put it up on the easel and get her a different color marker, too. She likes to have a new marker with a new piece of paper." I was hoping they got that straight because it could be hell to pay if you didn't do it just like Miss Susan was used to. But they were whispering back and forth to each other and not listening to me. They did not even say goodbye. What I think is, they may be real smart, but they are not real nice. So I just went on and left.

This suits me fine because I have decided it is time to go ahead and tell Willie about our baby. And then he will be so excited and want me to move right into the Tree House, which will be a relief because I have to say it is not good in the pink trailer anymore, even though I used to love it so at first. Tamika is all different now, she is moody and endangered, and Tony comes in and out pretty much whenever he wants to, he is not good for my baby, I can feel this in my bones as my grandma used to say. I know what she means now. Also I can feel my little baby girl inside me and I know it is time for us to leave.

So I'm all ready and excited to talk to Willie, but guess what, he is not at the Tree House when I get there even though his bike is chained out front to the porch rail. That means he is either running all over town in his red tennis shoes or he has gotten his mother's car out of that lot where she keeps it, we call it the car jail, and gone some place, now where could that be? This makes me feel kind of sick and bad but I go on in and sit down on the red futon sofa in the big room, next to the glass table that looks like a raindrop, it is a work of art, too. All of a sudden I feel like a birthday party balloon that all the gas has gone out of. Where is Willie? I don't know. I don't have any idea. Suddenly I realize that I don't have any idea about a lot of things—who Willie knows, where he goes when he isn't here, what he does when I'm not here, when I'm at work. I don't hardly know him, really. Well shoot I'm thinking, he might have a whole big life that I don't know anything about. This makes me feel like I'm falling. But I still feel closer to him than I have ever felt to anybody else in the whole world, ever. Sometimes when we are on that mattress I don't know where he stops and I start or anything, it's like he's a part of me. Of us, me and our baby.

So I just sit there on the futon with my ankles crossed and wait for him, like I am a lady in a painting, or like I'm waiting for a program or a play or something to start. And finally it does.

"Baby! Hey! What are you doing here? I thought you'd still be at work." Willie comes in looking different, he has on a nice blue shirt and loafers with his jeans, carrying his canvas bookbag.

"Well, I got off early," I say. "Miss Susan's children came, a surprise visit."

"Yeah?" That big sweet grin. "Well I've been thinking about you. I've got a surprise for you."

"I've got a surprise for you, too." I can't keep from smiling.

"Really? What is it?" He comes over and sits down on the sofa with me, putting his hand on my knee.

"You first," I say. I don't know why, but all of a sudden I'm scared to say it.

"Okay." Willie reaches for his canvas bag and pulls out something that looks like a catalog and a folder. "For you."

"Really?" I swear he is so sweet sometimes I just can't stand it. "What all have you got in there?"

"Well, look at it," Willie says, grinning. "Read it."

"Key West Community College," I read out loud. "Programs Offered." What in the world?

"I picked this up for you," Willie says. "I think you ought to go over to the college and take some of these classes. I think you'd love it, and I know they'd love to have you." I just look at him. He is serious.

"Oh, I couldn't do that," I say finally. My heart is just banging, hammering in my chest. I am filled with *trepidation* (word).

"Why not?"

"Well in case you haven't noticed, I've got a job, you silly thing," I say. "Actually I've got two jobs. I've got Miss Susan and I've got my mani-pedi ladies, too, whenever I can fit them in. But especially Miss Susan. What would Miss Susan do without me?"

"Honey, your Miss Susan isn't going to be here forever," Willie says gently. "In fact she's not going to be here much longer at all, you said so yourself. You said they're going to put her in a facility up in Del Ray, right?"

To my surprise I start crying. "I reckon," I say. All of a sudden I can't remember exactly. I know I've got this way of not paying attention to stuff I need to, Paula tried to help me with that.

"Well, honey," Willie says very sweet, "it seems to me that you have a natural talent for taking care of people, and I'm thinking maybe you ought to get one of those associate degrees in nursing and then you could get regular nursing jobs and have a real income from it. You could have health insurance. You wouldn't have to do nails."

"What do you mean? What are you talking about?" All of a sudden I was bawling. "I love to do nails. This is what I do. I told you, I'm an aesthetician!"

Willie smiles. Then he pulls back and takes my chin in his hand and looks at me good, real slow. "Of course you are, honey," he says. "But you're also a sweet and talented and very smart girl, and I'd like to do something for you. I'd like to send you back to school for one of these two-year associate degrees in nursing, if you want to go."

I start crying even more, because what Willie doesn't know is, there ain't no going back to school for me.

"I haven't been to school since the seventh grade," I tell him, "when I had to leave home in kind of a hurry. They wouldn't want me in that college place. No way."

"Oh, that's nothing," he says, all confident. "You can just get your GED first." Now he pulls out the other folder and hands it to me. "The GED is just a basic test, that's all, I bet you could ace it right now and then you can take any of these classes you want to. You can do anything in the world you want to do, Dee Dee. Anything. That's what I'm telling you. You're smart. Intelligent. Just think about it. I've been thinking about it myself. About you. And how hard you work, honey. I'd like to do something for you."

All of a sudden my heart starts beating real fast. There's something fishy about this, something I don't understand.

And then I do.

"You're leaving, aren't you?" I say. "You're going away, back where you came from." Of course he is, I'm thinking somewhere deep inside of me. I should of known he would. It was in the cards, in the stars, a done deal, *inevitable* (word).

He looked down at the floor. "I told you, you're smart. See how smart you are. But yeah, honey, my time here is just about up. My father is dying, out in California. I've got to go see him. And I've got to go back to graduate school."

At first I can't hardly say a word, I am speechless. "Thanks but no thanks," I tell him finally, "I'm not going to some school."

"Why not?"

I sit up real straight. "Because I'm having a baby. It's your baby, Willie. Yours and mine. That's what I'm going to do."

"Now you're kidding me, right?" Willie jumps up and starts walking around the room, real jittery all of a sudden. "Tell me you're not really pregnant. For God's sake, Dee Dee."

"I am so," I say. I stand up, too. "Here, you can feel her." I grab his hand and put it on my stomach, where you can almost feel the baby bump already.

"Shit," Willie says. "Goddamn it." He starts walking around and around the room and then comes back over to the sofa and sits down real close to me and takes both of my hands.

"Look, Dee Dee," he says, "You cannot have this baby. *We* cannot have this baby because there's not any 'we.' We are not a couple. We are not going to be a couple. We are two people whose lives crossed at a certain time, two people who found each other for a while, and we've had a great time, and I think the world of you. You've taught me a lot, honey. A lot about how to behave to other people—I think you are a truly good person—and a lot about how to grab every bit of joy out of life that you can. But I have to go back now. I have to see my father, and my extension is up. I have to go back to school now. And you have to have an abortion. I cannot be the father of this child, or any child, not now, not ever. I'm too, too fucked up and my life is too fucked up, my whole family is fucked up, don't you understand? I can't have a child. I can't do this, and I can't let you do it either." Now he's crying.

"You can't stop me," I hear myself say, because all of a sudden it's true. I want my baby more than I have ever wanted anything in my whole life before *ever*, I feel like this baby *is* me already, and I'm going to take such good care of her because I want her, I want to have a family, and I want something for myself, for me, Dee Dee! I feel powerful and invincible and omniscient or is it omnipotent (words), rising up up up the way I do, looking back down on Willie walking around and around down there like a crazy wind-up boy toy talking and talking. Maybe he *is* crazy, I'm thinking now, maybe *that*'s what's wrong with him, because there really *is* something wrong with him.

"Come on now, Dee Dee, You're a smart, lovely girl. You can have the life you deserve. I'll help you, of course. I swear I will. I'll pay for the abortion, the nursing degree, whatever I can do. Whatever you want. But you don't want to marry me, you really don't, you'd be better off with anybody else. Anybody, anybody at all, some guy on the street—that's what I'm trying to tell you. But I can fix this for you. I'll take care of you, I swear to God. I will. I can do that." He's walking and talking, crying and chattering, raking his hands through his hair.

I just watch him from where I am, way up high, a crazy boy walking around and around. I can look down and see everything and it's all small and colorful, the whole apartment, like it's made of LEGOs, and I can see myself down there, too, standing up, getting my things. The college stuff slides to the floor. I get my sweater and my pocketbook and my kit, that's all I take, and leave, I can see myself leave, a little LEGO girl, and him still talking. He follows her out the door and down the steps, still talking.

"We will take care of this honey," he says. "I'm going to take care of you." He's out there in the front yard still talking to me, a little LEGO boy red and blue, when I leave. "Come back, come back," he says.

"Oh I'll be in touch," I say, "I just need to go home now," as I float up and away. Willie just sits on the grass and puts his head down on his lap. Mister Chan is on the front porch doing tie chee, looking at him. I'm looking at him, too, a little LEGO boy I have misjudged, trusted, and loved. I float away in that sweet and gentle pale green rain that you get sometimes in the late afternoons in Key West.

Okay so maybe I am brokenhearted and *devastated* (word) but I am still my own self Dee Dee and I still have my own precious little baby girl and by God I am going to take care of her all by myself and she will be fine. We will be fine. All my life I have wanted something all my own and now I have her, mine to keep. Somewhere there's a place for us, I know. I just know it. I throw back my head and let it rain on my face and all over me, walking down Poor House Lane. It feels okay. It feels real good. Willie was always kind of crazy, I guess, and looking back now, I can see it. Maybe I always knew it. Sweet though. Willie was so so sweet. I feel like I was lucky to know him, and I'm lucky to have his baby, too. My baby. Fortunate. Fortuitous. (words).

I get the bus and go on back to the trailer and Tony is gone and Tamika has made some brownies out of a box and got some milk—"For you!" she says, hugging me. And so we sit down and eat them all up and drink the milk and then she starts singing that song we love so much from Frozen, "Let it go, let it go." We just wail it out and then Tamika sings "I Will Always Love You" just as good as Dolly, I swear, with her great big voice.

"Don't be scared of Tony," she says. "He's not so bad. He's helping me and he's gone help you, too, honey."

"No he's not. This is MY baby," I say.

Primary Colors

~~~~~~~~~~~~

Today it's a beautiful scene, like a French Impressionist painting. No: maybe Gauguin, or one of those Haitian paintings that Susan used to sell in her art gallery, or Louis's own work—primitive, colorful, fauve. Red and purple bougainvillea spills over the high pink stucco wall encircling the garden, buttonwood trees with their furry leaves form a silver hedge beneath. Notice the border of tropical plants: the prehistoric-looking elephant ear, the huge ferns, the big green cactus with all those spikes, the scary crown of thorns, the lignum vitae signifying death and, ironically, memory. Susan created this garden herself when Herbert Atlas bought her this home fifteen years ago. She used to delight in telling visitors, "See, look here—anything you'd think of as a house plant back home is a tree down here in Key West! Everything is enormous! Why, look at this bush, it's actually a coleus, just a little old coleus like the one I used to have in a pot on the windowsill in my kitchen. And look at this cactus—it could kill you! Can you believe it?"

Squares of emerald grass, trucked in fully grown and thriving, are lush and green as Ireland, thanks to an almost-invisible 24-hour sprinkler system, which works on a timer, like magic, now sprinkling the little butterfly garden to the side, with its Monarchs and Buckeyes and Swallowtails fluttering among the lantana and salvia they love, this butterfly garden being Susan's last addition to the garden before her onset—and all, all in the dappled shade of the giant strangler fig tree, its wide, leafy branches embracing everything. Susan sits at her easel enthralled, making swirls and slashes with an orange marker, Ashley and Abe in the Adirondack chairs observing her.

Ashley personally hates this outdoor garden, which she feels is too vivid—tasteless, lurid, and even dangerous—why, one of these plants is actually carnivorous! Susan said so herself! And today Susan is wearing a tacky turquoise sun hat with sequins on it, which Ashley would like to jerk right off her head. Ashley is absolutely sure that tacky little mani-pedi girl bought it for her. Probably at Wal-Mart! And really, this whole thing with the girl has gone on way too long already, it has gotten entirely out of hand. . . . Susan leans forward, clutching the easel with her left hand while she slashes and swipes at the paper with the orange marker in her right hand, biting her lip in concentration. (But can she actually concentrate? Isn't she too far gone?)

An awful thought comes to Ashley then, as unbidden as

the Monarch butterfly fluttering in the fragrant air before her. She grabs her husband's sleeve.

"Abe, honey, maybe we're making a mistake!" she whispers. "Maybe she's not as far gone as we thought. Did you think she could do this? Honestly now. Aren't you surprised?"

"Yes and no," Abe says in that calm, doctoral voice, which can always settle Ashley down.

"But we are not making a mistake, darling. You have to remember how much your stepmother always loved the arts—she was an artist herself, as I understand it, as well as a poet—for years before she became an art dealer, am I right? A very talented woman. We know that an appreciation for the arts remains longer than anything else as the illness progresses, probably because appreciation of the arts does not require cognition, if you follow me."

Ashley nods, both offended and relieved. Of course she can follow him. And of course he's right. He's always right. If she didn't love him so much, she'd hate him.

Dr. Abe continues. "So, in all ignorance I'm sure, this presumptuous young woman happened upon an activity for Susan that is actually deeply familiar, which is therefore comforting to her, therefore therapeutic. Primary colors within a frame. This would support recent studies showing that Alzheimer's patients in nursing homes can be calmed by listening to the music of their own era, familiar music, and also by participating in tasks and activities that they performed routinely in their own lives, such as folding towels and polishing silver for the women, raking leaves or washing a car for the men."

"Really!" Ashley squeezes her husband's manicured hand. She knows he has never washed a car in his life.

> Orange and black is the color of butterfly wings
> Monarch!
> He is beautiful
> He can do anything
> He can cross continents
> He will crash and burn
> Black is the color of dead
> White is the color of gone

Suddenly Susan slumps back in her chair as if exhausted, eyes brimming. She flings her orange-marked paper to the grass.

"Gone," she says clearly.

Dr. Abe leans forward. "It's all right, Susan," he says in the Voice of God.

But Ashley jumps up to hug her stepmother and is so excited to feel a similar pressure from Susan, a thin arm hugging her back. "Don't worry," Ashley reassures her, "I've got another piece of paper for you right here, see, look, I'll put it up on the easel for you. There. Now. And here's a new marker for you, too. Green."

Immediately Susan is absorbed again, not even looking up as Maribeth and Pat join the group, stopping well back yet still within the canopy of the strangler fig.

"Hi Mama," Maribeth calls gently, entering the garden,

but Susan does not even look up, biting her lip. She's making loops with the green marker.

"Isn't this amazing?" Ashley turns to ask.

"Well I don't know whether to shit or go blind!" Pat announces in her gravelly Southern voice.

Everybody laughs, a relief.

"So where's Miss Va Va Voom?" Pat asks.

"I told her that she could leave early, I wanted us to be able to observe Susan ourselves, without her. The next Home Health nurse will be here in about—" Dr. Abe looks at his Rolex—"thirty minutes now. So we can observe freely until then."

Pat goes over to the round table and comes back with two chairs, which she places near the others.

Maribeth sinks down in hers, suddenly exhausted. "It's so green out here, isn't it?" she says dreamily, "almost like it's fake grass."

Pat snorts. "Everything's fake in Florida, haven't you noticed?" She, for one, has had enough of it! She's ready to get back to Cleveland.

"Green, green, it's green they say, on the far side of that hill," Maribeth sings softly. She thought she'd be a folksinger once, and she still has a beautiful voice. "Green, green, I'm going away to where the grass is greener still . . ."

Susan is making a garden.

Green
Garden
Ireland

Key West
Lizard
Little frog
Salad
Grass
Graves

Susan throws her paper down on the grass.

"Oh no," Maribeth says. "I'm afraid we upset her by coming in late. Or talking too much. Or me singing—oh, I'm so sorry."

Susan throws her marker on the grass, too, followed by her hat, which catches the breeze and sails a few feet away. Her blond hair is wild, spiky, standing straight up. Now she's making a humming sound.

"I don't like that noise," Pat says, standing up.

"Oh sit down. She just wants some more paper, that's what Renee said, keep giving her more paper. Here, honey." Ashley jumps up to put a new sheet on the easel. She hands Susan another marker. Purple.

Hunching her back, Susan leans forward in her chair, her face very close to the easel. She makes hard jabbing dots and slashing marks on the paper. It's as if the rest of them are not there at all. Then she starts humming again.

"What in the world happened to her hair?" Ashley asks. It looks atrocious, frightening. At the Atrium, there's a very nice beauty parlor/barber shop to keep all the patients looking as nice as possible. The beauticians will even come to your room. Appearance is important, Abe says. Therapeutic.

"Renee did her hair," Maribeth says. "Cut and color, sort of a pixie. It looked pretty good at first. It's growing out now."

Susan just keeps humming, louder and louder.

"Mama, Mama, what's wrong, honey?" Maribeth cries, coming forward, arms out to help.

Purple is the color of people I hate

~~~~~~~~~~~~~~~~

Thrown with surprising force, the wooden easel catches Maribeth on the temple, opening up a gash, which bleeds profusely as Maribeth stumbles and falls to the emerald grass.

"Honey!" Pat leaps to her side, pulling her up. Blood streaks through Maribeth's long blond hair now, running down her face and onto her white peasant blouse.

"Oh my God!" Ashley hides her face against her husband's shoulder.

"Calm down, everyone, just calm down," Dr. Abe intones. "Head wounds are famously, deceptively bloody. Don't worry. I'm sure there is no real harm done."

"No harm done, my ass!" Pat, furious, leads Maribeth away to the car, heading straight for the Urgent Care out Flagler Avenue.

"Now Susan," Dr. Abe says in his most commanding voice, standing up to his full six feet five inches. "It's all right. There's nothing to be afraid of." Carefully he moves toward

Susan, who's now backed up against the smooth trunk of the giant tree. There's nowhere else for her to go. He stretches his long arms out, opening them wide. "Come to me. You are safe, Susan. You are here at home in your own garden. At your own home. Come to me."

Susan hums louder and louder. "Rat-a-tat-tat! Rat-a-tat-tat!" she chants, then runs forward, picks up her garden chair and hurls it at him, hitting him on the shoulder. Dr. Abe staggers backward but only for a moment, already reaching into his little shoulder pack for the hypodermic.

AFTERNOON DRIFTS AWAY through the garden. The breeze comes up, ruffling the silver leaves of the buttonwood trees, skidding the glittery turquoise hat along the grass until it comes to rest in the tangled fronds of a huge Boston fern, out of sight. Nobody in this story will ever find it. Round red leaves fall from the Seagrape tree near the big house, spangling the grass. Susan used these leaves for plates at the garden parties she used to have for her granddaughters and their dolls, years ago. The sun sets, the shadows deepen, the wind comes up to make a sighing sound like music in the vast canopy of the sheltering strangler fig tree. Little lights along the walkways turn on automatically.

"Hey, anybody home?" Herb yells, pushing through the gate at seven thirty after Ricky drops him off from his chemo treatment up in Marathon. "Hey, hey Renee! What's happening, baby!" They told him he would feel tired, or nauseous, but he doesn't. He's starving. That's what, they're trying to starve him to death. Be a helluva lot easier for everybody.

The hell with 'em. He feels fine, just fine, but where the hell *is* everybody? "Maribeth!" he yells. "Pat! What the fuck!"

But no one is here, and it looks to Herb like no one has ever been here at all, the easel gone, the chairs placed back around the table. The little house, Susan's house, is dark. Her garden rustles, sighs, and breathes, wild and lovely in the slanted dying light, keeping its secrets.

Packing Up

~~~~~~~~~~~~~~~~~~~~~~~~~~~~~~~~~

"Everybody loves the hukilau. . . ." The doorbell rings again and again through the stately rooms of the big pink house as all these goddamn people come and go, come and go until it's driving him nuts and finally Herbert Atlas reaches up and rips the goddamn thing out of the wall, leaving an ugly hole. Who cares? But then he thinks, oh shit, the girl, not-Renee, didn't he leave her a message to come over, what if she comes now and nobody hears her at the door? He sits down heavily in his big plaid chair, now out here in the Atrium because they're sending it up to Del Ray for him, along with his painting of the rampaging rhino by that guy . . . Ford, what's his name? Well shit. He can't remember a goddamn thing these days. He scoots the chair closer to the window so maybe he can see her coming if she comes. If he sent her that message, he can't remember.

"Oh Pop!" Maribeth sighs as she looks up from sealing a box of old papers, documents from the big secretary, which used to be Susan's business desk. "Now we'll just have to hire somebody to come over here and fix that." Her dad is just like a nine-year-old, only worse. In fact he's gotten a lot worse since Abe had Susan transferred up to Del Ray in that impressive white van with THE ATRIUM embossed in gold on the sides, but tasteful, along with the pretty ring of blooming flowers, the Atrium's seal. The uniformed driver had backed the van expertly up to the house, honestly it could have been a floral delivery truck. The back doors opened smartly as two hale and hearty nurse types jumped out, an athletic-looking young man and a smiling middle-aged nurse.

They followed Ashley into the house with a rolling hospital bed, which they lowered from the van, then emerged about thirty minutes later with Susan on it sweetly sleeping her drug-induced sleep, wearing a pretty robe, all tucked in. The bed was lifted mechanically into the back of the van; luggage was stowed in another compartment. Ashley took her place in the chair at Susan's side while the nurse—her name was Joyce—sat on Susan's other side checking her blood pressure. Ashley would ride back to Del Ray in the van, then stay. Ricky would drive Herb up a few days later. Susan looked comfortable, pretty, at rest. She had not been at rest for so long. It all happened smoothly, in no time at all. Joyce waved and smiled as the doors slid shut. Ashley threw kisses from the van, like she was in a parade. That van was reassuring, though Maria, back in the doorway, cried with her hand to her face.

Maribeth is sure the Atrium is perfectly fine, and honestly, what else could they do? Everyone is in agreement—everyone except Herb, of course. He's being just as difficult as humanly possible.

At first, right after they took Susan away, Herb wouldn't have anything to do with it, any of it, packing or closing up his house. He sat in the rec room in the dark watching the Masters Golf Tournament in Augusta, on the giant wall TV, all those beautiful long green fairways, perfectly groomed, the slanting sun, the beautiful flowers, the flags, the crowd. There's nothing like Augusta, the Old South. Pretty blond women, manners. Gracious. Shit. Herbert Atlas never played golf in his life. But watching the Masters calmed him down and kept him out of everybody else's hair for four days. He's always for Phil Mickelson, Phil's getting kind of long in the tooth now and he's got some fucking disease, what is it, he's always talking about it on TV, but he's a gentleman, always a gentleman. Yeah. Herb also likes Dustin Johnson and Tiger Woods, who also likes pussy a little too much, yeah Herb can relate to that. He hates Sergio García, who luckily missed the cut. Finally Phil wins. Good. He's kissing his wife, those cute kids. Augusta is always good. The way life should be.

Maribeth sighs. Today, with the Masters over, Herb is worse than ever, ripping the doorbell from the wall and insisting on sitting in his big chair right here in the middle of the living room where people are trying to get things done. It's sad, of course it's sad, but it will be a relief when Ricky comes tomorrow to drive him up to the Atrium, too. They're already done with him here. He's put his unreadable signature on everything requiring his signature, his clothes have been packed and sent to Del Ray already. He won't need much, so most are headed to Goodwill where nobody will really appreciate them, Maribeth knows, she wept as she folded those expensive dinner jackets and suits that Susan had tailor-made for him, what did he care? What did he ever care about clothes? He looks like hell all the time anyway, Maribeth can't imagine that's going to change at the Atrium. He'll probably go around in his pajama pants all the time there, too, she packed plenty of those for him. Damnit, she's crying again.

"How ya doin' today, Pop?" Pat stops beside Herb's chair to give him a hug. She's the only one he doesn't snap at, the only one he'll put up with at all. "Whatcha doin'? You got a delivery coming? You waiting for somebody?" She winks at Maribeth.

Pat thinks this is a joke, ha! Herb just grunts in response.

Pat was born for this, wearing that kind of apron like they wear in Home Depot, with numerous tools and tags and stickers in the big front pockets, carrying an impressive clipboard with the changing tasks and needs of each day, each hour at the forefront. Command central. Maribeth shakes her head. How did Pat know how to do this? How to get a big house ready to sell? How to dismantle a household? And dismantle the lives inside? But nothing overwhelms Pat, or even fazes her. It's all about organization, says Pat, who used to be the dean of an engineering school and then ran the entire transit system in Cincinnati. After that, there's nothing to it, nothing to anything. Pat—the person that phrase "heart of gold" was invented for.

Maribeth loves Pat's cap of thick sandy hair, graying now, her freckles, her flashing grin, her sturdy build, her purposeful walk, oh what is the word? Her *stride*. Maribeth sighs. What in the world would this family do without Pat? What would *she* have done? She smiles, remembering. How much she needed that humor, that organization and strength when they first met, when Maribeth moved into a condominium next door, a brand-new divorcée with two jittery little daughters and no job and no notion of how or where to get one. Her young husband had just left her, simply packed a bag and walked out the door with no explanation whatsoever. Dave—weren't they all named Dave then? She'd married the first one that asked her.

Pat moves on. "Sandwiches from Five Brothers coming at noon for lunch," she tosses back over her shoulder. Pat has always believed in feeding everybody she employs, a technique that works wonders. And this is the packers' last day—wearing uniforms with their names on their pockets—Angie, Don, Beth, Shorty—which makes them look like a singing quartet, or the cast of a Broadway show or something . . . like they might burst into song at any moment. Now they're down to the silver and the glassware in the huge armoire in the dining room and the serving pieces in the butler's pantry, wrapping each spoon, each fork, each tray meticulously . . . though who wants silver anymore? Nobody in this family apparently, except Dr. Abe, who suddenly spoke up. Who knew? Pat smiles, shaking her head. He's a case, Abe. What's he gonna do with all this silver? Sell it, probably. Or have a coronation dinner for himself? But who cares? Pat can't wait to get back to their own real life, to Cincinnati.

She checks the clipboard. She winks at Ricky, who slides

through this busy scene from time to time like a fish swimming in and out of a coral reef, weaving between the people and boxes and displaced furniture, touching a shoulder here, there, making a joke with Herb in his chair. He's the only one who can handle Herb, and everybody knows it.

Maribeth tapes up the last box of documents from the mammoth secretary, closes the final drawer, stands up, stretches. Her back is killing her. She thought it would make her so sad to close up the old family home, this beautiful house, but actually it is not beautiful at all now with the art gone, all packed up and taken away with great care by the special packers from Sotheby's. Rumors floated that the big Chihuly sculpture alone might be worth a million. The family has chosen some of the art, of course. Ashley and Abe are taking the bigger, more formal paintings, and all the garden statuary, for the Atrium. Boxes have been packed and sent to New York, Jacksonville, Cincinnati. . . . Pat doesn't give a damn about the art, but Maribeth has carefully made a selection for the two of them. They don't have room for these paintings now, of course, but they'll probably buy a second home down South someplace themselves, maybe on one of those golf resorts around Charleston, S.C., also a great place for children and grandchildren and nieces and nephews to visit. Pat has a sister and brother, too. Why, they'll have their own family home! Maribeth finds herself crying.

Susan's little house is already empty, cleaned, and locked. Pat gave all that furniture to Maria and her family, except for the puffy chair and the easel, which are already at the Atrium with Susan, along with a couple of small botanical prints and that jungle-looking painting by Louis, which she loved, and a big box of family photographs, which Maribeth packed very carefully, though Susan will probably never recognize any of those people again, any of them, her family. Maribeth just couldn't help it, she sent that box along to the Atrium in the white van anyway, the box filled with Susan's whole life.

Last Visit

~~~~~~~~~~~~~~~~~~~~~~~~~~~~~~

In spite of everything, Dee Dee feels pretty good, walking over to the pink house for the last time to tell Mr. Atlas goodbye. She just naturally feels good, for one thing, and even though Willie will be leaving soon, she's got a baby and she's got a line on another job and she's got some money, too. Mrs. Dunlap, the old lady on down Washington Street in the big concrete house, has had a bad fall and needs several people to come in and help her when she gets out of the hospital, and Miss Maribeth has recommended *her*, Dee Dee! She's got an interview with Mrs. Dunlap's son on Monday. The money came from Ricky, more money than she has ever had in her life, also a lot of advice, which Dee Dee is determined to follow.

Ricky had called her on her cell phone and said he'd pick her up in front of the trailer park, that Mr. Atlas wanted him to settle up with her.

"Okay," she'd said, although they'd already paid her every

time she'd come, but then she almost died because all this time she'd thought they didn't know where she lived. She'd been so careful. And if Ricky knew this, what else did he know?

A *lot*, it turned out.

He picked her up in that little red car she'd always secretly loved and then took her to the Green Parrot Bar and ordered a beer for himself and a ginger ale for her and some guacamole and chips and salsa, which was just great because she was starving. "Sweet Caroline" was playing on the jukebox, a song she's always loved. Then Ricky put a brown envelope on the table in front of her. The envelope had her real name printed out on it in big letters, MISS DEIRDRE JUNE MULLINS. Her face got real hot all of a sudden, looking at it, and then she looked up at him, that handsome dark face like some dude on TV. He kept his hat on. He was grinning at her, white white teeth. She had reached out for the chips and then stopped, stock still, frozen, but now he leaned across the table and took her hand, holding it gently but firmly.

"Listen, Miss Deirdre Mullins from North Carolina," he said, "*Dee Dee*. I'm on to you. You did a good job here, honey, and you got away with it, but you need to go ahead and disappear now, get out of here while the getting is good. You need to clean up your act, start over, use your real name, get a real job, and take care of that baby or get rid of it."

Dee Dee felt hot and awful, looking at the envelope. Like she was getting sick. "Does Mr. Atlas know about all this?" she finally asked. "Miss Pat? Miss Maribeth?"

"Nope." He studied her seriously, like a judge or a minister.

"Nobody knows this. Nobody knows anything about you, how you got here or what you've been through."

"So what *is* this, then?" she pushed at the envelope. "Sweet Caroline" was so peppy, it was making her crazy.

"Money," he said. "Quite a lot of it."

"But they don't owe me any money," she said. "They paid me cash, all the way. I'm all paid up."

"Consider it a bonus." Ricky released her hand then and took a sip of his beer so she took a drink of her ginger ale, too, and then she started crying and laughing at the same time and spilled her ginger ale all over the place. "Oh I'm so sorry," she said. "I'm just a nut."

"No, you're not," Ricky said, wiping it all up. "You're a smart girl, so you're going to do what I'm telling you, all right?"

She nodded.

"Put this money someplace safe, right now. Open a bank account, put it in the bank."

Dee Dee didn't know what to say. She opened her mouth and then closed it, staring at him. "I can't do that," she said finally. "I don't really have an address, right now anyhow. I'm going to be moving real soon though."

Ricky smiled at her, big toothshine in the shade of his hat. "Well, I'm damn glad to hear that, honey. But let me tell you something. You know that mailing place in Duval Square, right off Simonton, real near Rite Aid where you get the bus? It's across the courtyard from the sushi bar."

She nodded, heart pounding. That's exactly where she

went with Willie to help him mail his boxes of books back to Boston.

"Okay. Well, they've also got safeboxes in there, a lot of them that you can rent, just like you can rent one of their mailboxes if you don't have an address. Short-term or long-term. I think you ought to rent both, right now. Then you'll have a safe place to put your money and a place where you can get mail, too. An address."

Dee Dee just opened her mouth and closed it. She didn't know any of this stuff.

"I'm pulling for you, honey. You can do this. I know you've had a hard time, but I know you're a good girl. A smart girl. And I believe in you." He stuck out his hand.

Dee Dee's heart was banging in her chest as she took it. He was being real sweet but how much did he know? And *what* did he know? She never should of let Tamika talk her into getting those pills.

Ricky gave her a hard handshake, like she was a boy or a man. It made her feel good. He left a little business card in her palm. "Get in touch," he said. "If you need to."

Then he drove her home in style, raising dust in the lot at the trailer park when he swerved around and slammed on the brakes. He got out on his side and came around to her side and opened the door for her like a gentleman and then took her hand and kissed it with a little bow. Dee Dee started giggling, she just couldn't help it. Miss Violet waved from her chair in front of the Airstream, and the old couple in the green trailer peered out to look, too. Dee Dee waved at everybody, clutching the envelope against her baby under the tunic. *Damn!*

So now she's staying in the abandoned green camper at the end of the row of trailers, under the gumbo limbo tree, paying Tony a hundred dollars a week. The camper is real old and real little but she cleaned it out good and bought herself new sheets and pillows at Walmart for the pulldown bed and a battery fan and two electric lanterns and a cooler at Lowe's right up the street, paying cash for everything. Whew. That's all so far. It's all they need, her and her baby, while she figures out what to do next. Her clothes and her nail stuff and everything else is all jammed in there, it's cute really. It is okay for now, they won't be here long. Next on her list is to go to that mail place on Duval Square. For now the envelope is safe under the mattress of the pull-down bed. Some days she thinks she's going to name the baby Ariel, other days she thinks Tiana. Princess names. She also likes the name Antonia, like the restaurant down on Duval Street.

But she can't help thinking about William, which she seems to be calling him now, like he's somebody else, like he's already gone, someplace far away. He almost is. He's mostly gone already, though their lovemaking is more passionate than ever before, almost desperate, sometimes she is afraid he will hurt the baby. He's still on it about the baby and all that school stuff. He is *obstinate* (word). There is a way in which William, sweet as he is, just cannot understand that everything won't be the way he wants it to be. That's all he has ever known, Dee Dee understands now. So she just goes way way up above her head whenever he starts talking this stuff. But weirdly she loves him even more, every little bit of him, from those big ugly glasses to his ribs and collarbone that stick out and his knobby knees and his beautiful voice like a movie star when he reads poems out loud to her such as E. E. Cummings and that old Irish guy, she wishes he would not do this though she loves to hear him read the poems. This just makes it all harder. He still can't believe he can't get her to do what he wants, why would he think any different? He is just a boy. She has kept that community college stuff though, maybe she'll do that someday anyway. Who knows *what* she might do! She's on her way now.

So Dee Dee smiles, walking down Washington Street for the very last time to tell Mr. Atlas goodbye. It's the least she can do!

But she stops short when she sees the number of vehicles parked all along the front sidewalk. It looks like the whole place is full of people. There's a FedEx truck, a huge moving van with the back door open and the ramp down, a delivery van from Five Brothers, Miss Pat's Honda Odyssey with the Ohio plates, and four or five cars she can't identify. Lord! But at least Ricky's little red sports car is not here, he might get mad at her for coming over. Dee Dee starts down the front walkway just as the Five Brothers delivery guy comes out the door. He says, "Well hello there, honey!" as he passes her, too close, on the sidewalk. Dee Dee has almost reached the entrance when something tells her to look up and then she sees him *looming* (word) there at the window, that wild old man. He nods his head and jerks his thumb toward the side.

Okay. That's a relief actually. Dee Dee takes the flagstone path around the house to the right, the way she always came to work. Good. She wants to take one more look at Miss Susan's garden anyway.

But the picket gate turns out to be locked. Tears come to her eyes even though she should have known it would be. The garden beyond is as green and shady and cool and peaceful as ever. The butterflies flutter around the little butterfly garden, the wind sighs through that big old tree that Miss Susan loved so. The roses and daylilies and all the other flowers keep right on blooming like crazy, they don't give a damn that Miss Susan's gone. Well, Dee Dee gives a damn. She gives a great big damn! She loved Miss Susan and she knows Miss Susan loved her even if she couldn't say it.

Dee Dee holds her left hand up in the sunshine turning it this way and that, admiring the charms on Miss Susan's silver bracelet that she had when she was a girl, Miss Maribeth said when she gave it to Dee Dee. These were all the things of her life then: a little silver pony, a heart, a musical note, an *S* for *Susan*, some kind of rolled-up thing like a newspaper—Dee Dee can't remember what Miss Maribeth said that was—a high-heel shoe, and one of those artist things with little jewels on it like dabs of paint, red, blue, green, bright as the sun, which shines now on this garden as happily as ever, like a warm smile.

She hears Mr. Atlas huffing and puffing before he even gets there, coming around the japonica bush at the corner wearing his favorite T-shirt, which says *If You Can Read This, the Bitch Fell Off* on the back and some baggy black sweatpants and some brand-new tennis shoes, somebody must have bought him the sweatpants and the tennis shoes for his move to the Atrium. He looks pretty much the same, even though he's real sick now.

"Hi Mr. Atlas," she says.

"Hi yourself," Mr. Atlas says, rough as ever, though Dee Dee knows he's not mean, he's nice.

"Where are you going, dressed like that? Are you going to a health club?" She giggles, and then she is real upset, *mortified* (word) that maybe she's hurt his feelings.

"I ain't going no place," he snaps. "Just taking a little walk around my yard, around my *property*, soon to be somebody else's property." He reaches out and rattles the lock on the picket fence. "Fuck it! I shoulda known. Locked out."

Dee Dee nods. "It's real sad. But I'll never forget this garden. I'll never forget Miss Susan either, she was always so sweet to me. I'm so glad you invited me to come over here today, I really wanted to thank you in person for everything, and I really wanted to see the garden one more time." And I will never forget it as long I live, Dee Dee is thinking, the way it was here. Never.

What? What the fuck? He'll be damned if he invited this girl not-Renee to come over here. Herb puts his hands on his hips, looking all around at the garden, at the fence, back at the house, thinking hard. Real hard. And then it just comes to him, out of the blue, out of nowhere. Shit. Why not?

"C'mere," he says, leading her by the hand toward the big triple garage. But can he remember the code? Shit. And then he *does* remember, 6666, six was always a good number for him, he always bet on six or any multiple of six. . . . The garage door rumbles up.

"Well, come on, then!" He pulls the girl by the elbow, surprisingly hard, and the door rumbles down behind him. There now. Nobody knows where they are. Nobody.

"C'mere, honey, I wanna show you something." He starts pulling the blue acrylic cover off the Porsche, his beloved yellow Porsche, which he hasn't even seen in how long? Three years? Two years at least. Damn thing probably won't even run now.

"Oh my goodness, Mr. Atlas! Let me help you. Here!" She drops her big silver purse on the cement floor and starts pulling, too, it's some kind of very high-tech material, like a shiny second skin, but it slides right off to make a puddle on the cement floor. "Why, what in the world? What kind of a car *is* this? It looks like a car in a movie!" She runs her hand along the side. "P-O-R-S-C-H-E," she spells out loud. "Porch!" Now she's giggling, that childlike giggle he loves. "I have never in my whole life heard of a car named for a porch!"

He guffaws, then pronounces it correctly for her. "French," he says. "It's French or German or some kind of shit. It was made in Europe someplace. It's a foreign language." He used to know this, of course. Shit.

But the girl is clapping her hands, delighted. "Well, I swan," she says. "I never saw anything like this."

"I bought it for Susan, my bride. She just loved it. I used to drive her all around town in it, she'd wear a scarf and I'd wear my Panama hat, she waved at everybody. Everybody. And they waved back."

She claps her hands again at the idea of Susan, the Susan she knew, riding around the crowded little streets of Key West as a bride. "Oh I would have given anything to see that!"

"Yeah?" he squints at her.

Her face gives off light like the sun.

"So whaddya think, honey? You wanna take a little ride?"

Now she draws back. "Oh, Mister Atlas, you know you're not supposed to drive, are you? And this car has been all covered up and everything . . ."

He just laughs, fingering the Porsche keys in the money pouch at his belt, the keys he found in his two-tone golf shoes. "I tell you what, sugar. Let's just see if it runs, and then I'll drive you home. Then you won't have to take the bus, how's that?"

Her eyes light up and the big smile covers her whole face.

He clicks the key and the passenger door opens, all by itself.

"Oh gosh, look at that!" She grabs up her silver bag and slides into the passenger seat, slamming the door behind her.

Herb presses the key to open his door, but can he even get in there now? This is the question. And if he does get in, can he ever get out? It's so low. . . .

"Come on, Mister Atlas," she cries out, "You can do it!"

He does it, settling himself. He's lost some weight lately, since he got sick, so he still fits, just barely, son of a gun. He needs his hat, his shades. Too late now. Okay, this is the big time. He turns the key in the ignition and the engine roars.

She squeals like a kid. Well, she is a kid.

"Okey dokey, let's go!" Okey dokey is an expression she learned from old ladies, from doing their nails.

Herb backs the Porsche out, makes a perfect three-point turn in the paved area in front of the garage, then heads out slowly into the street. Nobody's noticing, he's sure. He points out the red Five Brothers van to the girl. "See that? That's the Cuban sandwiches from Five Brothers. Good. Everybody's eating their lunch."

"Oooh, I wish I had one!"

"We'll pick something up on the way," Herb tells her, switching gears. The car purrs like a cat. "Atta girl," he says, leaning back, putting on the sunglasses, which are still right there in the console between the seats. Ray-Bans. The best of everything. Shit yeah! He hasn't lost a thing.

Road Trip

~~~~~~

Oh my God! is all I can think driving down Washington Street in the fancy little porch car with old Mister Atlas at the wheel, with his mirror shades! I get the giggles and can't stop. And then he's rooting around in that box thing between our seats, and he pulls a baseball cap out of there and puts it on, red and white, PHILLIES it says. It looks real old. "So are you a Phillies fan?" I ask him and he says, "Hell no, honey, I hate the Phillies. This is my disguise, get it?" which gets me laughing, I swear he is the funniest old man.

So I root around in my own bag and take out my silver sequin baseball cap and my sunglasses. "Ta-da!" I say, "me too!" and my reward is his big old grin.

"So where are we going?" I ask.

And he says, "Wherever you want to go. Let's take a little drive. Where do you want to go?"

Which just throws me because nobody has ever has asked me that before, in fact one thing I have never had in my whole life is my own transportation though there's a lot of other things I have never had either. Such as my own *destination* (word). So I sit back in the seat and say, "Well let's just take a little drive then," because I know we'll have to get back real soon, he's not supposed to drive at all, but I can't wipe this big smile off my face because this is all so crazy. That is one thing about Mister Atlas, you don't ever know what he is going to say or do next. He is *impromptu* (word).

Now we're riding along Smathers Beach with swimmers and sunbathers and people standing up on those boogie boards in the water (how do they do that?) and flying big, huge, colorful kites and even flying way up in the air on the kites themselves while being pulled along by a little boat with ropes. "Omigod," I say, "Look at that! I would never do that!" and Mister Atlas makes a snorting noise and says, "Crazy kids will do anything."

I have never been to this beach myself but I didn't mind so much because I don't know how to swim and sun is real bad for your complexion anyway, everybody knows that, but now I'm thinking, wait a minute—it looks like so much fun out there, with all the stands renting beach chairs and selling food, popcorn and hot dogs and sno-cones—what is a sno-cone? The other side of the highway is nothing but huge high-rise hotels, one after the other, and fancy restaurants such as Benihana (Japanese) and La Trattoria (Italian), and when we slow down for traffic, we're right next to two guys walking along with their arms around each other for all to see. I'm thinking that if anybody did this up home, they would both get shot. But Key West is full of them, along with signs that say GAY ONLY and ALL ARE WELCOME.

"Jesus Christ, would you look at that? Right out in public!" Mister Atlas makes that snorting noise.

"All are welcome," I say, and then we both just die laughing.

"I'll say one thing for you honey," Mister Atlas says. "You know how to have a good time. You could make lemonade out of lemons, that's a good trait in a person."

What is a <u>trait</u>? I make a note in my head.

We drive past the West Martello Tower, some historic old fort next to the airport where I can see planes flying in and out. I have never been on a plane but I want to. I want to do everything. We drive around a wide bend, huge condos on the land side and the water on the other, no beach now but a mangrove swamp with open sea beyond, and a whole community of houseboats bobbing up and down in the water. "Oh I would love to live on one of those!" I say out loud without meaning to, remembering how I always used to dream about running away from home, like if we went on a road trip to Asheville I would pick out the old barns and the mountains with caves in them, or any place along the highway where I could hide, a place for me, Dee Dee. That was even before Mama got so sick, and way before she died.

There's a stoplight up ahead. "Okay honey," Mister Atlas says as we approach it. "We gotta make a decision here. You wanna turn down Truman and go home, that's the closest way. Or you wanna drive all around the island on Roosevelt and then go home?"

All of a sudden right there is Bare Assets, the strip club on Truman, which is the place the guys dropped me and Tamika off when we first got down here to Key West, right there in the parking lot of Bare Assets, which is where Jude worked, that was one of their girlfriends, she's the one that took us over to the trailer park. But we couldn't even try to get a job at Bare Assets ourselves because it is sort of high class and you have to look good, you have to have the right clothes to apply for a job to take them all off, I know that sounds crazy but it's true. We didn't have a thing but what was on our backs. Lord! I have to close my eyes for a minute.

I don't know what got into me then but all of a sudden I open my eyes and say, "What about that way?" pointing to the right where the sign says ROUTE ONE. OVERSEAS HIGHWAY.

Mister Atlas's big old bushy eyebrows shoot up and he turns around to look at me good. "You mean Stock Island? You wanna go over to Stock Island, baby? "

"Well, whatever is out there," I said. "I mean, as long as we're just taking a ride." Actually I don't have a clue what is out there because we had been closed up in the back of a moving van the entire time, me and Tamika riding down here to get away from the program. She'd fucked a boy to get us a ride. We couldn't see the water or the Keys or anything. Tamika and me sat in the dark on a pile of canvas bags that they use to cover furniture and we talked and sang and carried on the whole way when we weren't asleep. They let us out to pee in the dark on the side of the road a couple of times and got us some Cokes and hot dogs at a gas station with the last of our money. Then all of a sudden we were here, Key

West, and the boy that was driving pulled into the lot behind Bare Assets and they opened the big door and the sun was blinding and they said, "Go, go! Get out of here!" and the girl Jude was there, too, and she said, "Well you can't just kick them out like that" and then she said, "Well, shit. Come on with me."

Mister Atlas laughed and turned his blinker on. Right. "You got it, sweet chips," he said. He's always calling me these crazy names. He drove across a bridge. MM5 the sign said. "Now you're on Stock Island." Which didn't look too different from Key West to me, only cheaper, and tackier. *Seedier* is the word. Signs said LAZY DOG ADVENTURES and CHICO'S CANTINA and PADDLEBOARD TOURS and GOLF CLUB, which must be where Miss Pat used to come to play golf all the time, I bet she was pretty good at it. She said she had a low handicap though I couldn't see she had any handicap at all. I really liked Pat, I'm thinking, then I realize I'm thinking about it all like it happened way in the past, a long time ago, and it's all over now. Then we stop for a light and I see this little green sign on the left that says COLLEGE ROAD and another bigger, fancier sign that says KEY WEST COMMUNITY COLLEGE, and all of a sudden my heart starts beating real fast like I'm having a heart attack and my eyes fill up with tears behind my sunglasses, I just can't help it.

Mister Atlas is looking at me. "You had enough, honey? Or you wanna go a little bit farther up the Keys?"

"Up the Keys," I say, and he laughs and pushes the gas pedal and then we're over the water on a big bridge heading for Boca Chica Key, aqua blue water spread out on either side of us as far as the eye can see, dotted with little islands. It is the most beautiful thing I have ever seen. Then we're on Big Coppitt Key and planes are flying over us, it's like they are dive-bombing us.

"US Naval Air Station," Mister Atlas says. "Very important. Very strategic. Don't be scared, they're just doing exercises."

On we go up the ribbon of road until Mister Atlas says, "Oh oh," and then, "Well, shit," and then pulls into the worst-looking gas station you have ever seen, at Mile Marker 10 on Cudjoe Key. "Sorry honey. I just noticed that red Empty sign and I figure I'd better gas up here before we get on any more long bridges. It would be hell to run out of gas on one of these bridges."

"I can fill it up," I say, but he says, "Hell no, I've gotta pee anyway of course," and then I get really worried because I'm thinking he will never be able to get out of the car. I mean it's real low to the ground, and sure enough it's really really hard for him until finally a nice big Cuban guy comes over and pulls him out and then Mister Atlas does this sad, slow sort of walk around to the restroom, limping and stumbling. That's when I know, all of a sudden, I've got to get him back home. I've got to. But I have to pee myself, and I have to say, that bathroom is just awful, a life-changing experience as Miss Pat said one time when things got bad at Miss Susan's little house though this seems like years ago, another lifetime. Things get even worse when I come out to find Mister Atlas having a big argument with the station guy because the pump won't work.

Meanwhile the other side of the pump is tied up by a big

old station wagon full of Cubans who are having the best time, they have all gotten out while the one guy is filling the car up, and they're playing the radio real loud, some kind of Cuban music, I think you say mariachi, and some of them go in the station while two boys and a girl start dancing right here on the pavement, having so much fun I want to join them. I love this kind of music myself.

"What the fuck! What the fuck!" Mister Atlas comes back yelling, hitching up his sweatpants, but nobody can hear him. He goes on and has a real hissy fit but nobody cares. The rest of the Cubans come out with beer and nachos and chips and stuff, and now it's a party. Mister Atlas is about to die. I mean really die. His face is dark red.

"You shouldn't get so mad," I tell him. "You're going to have a heart attack." I know he takes heart pills along with all his other pills.

"I'm not mad, I'm frustrated!" he yells.

The Cubans keep on dancing. So I think what the hell, I just go over there and start dancing with them and they all yell and clap and give Mister Atlas a beer, which he chugs, to my surprise, and then the cute boy with the moustache pumps our gas for us, and Mister Atlas gives him some money from the money belt, and everybody's grinning by the time we pull out.

"You're right, honey," he says. "I gotta calm down some. I gotta smell the roses," though there are not any actual roses out here on Route 1 so I guess this is an image, a word picture as in a poem, like Willie told me. He also told me he will be leaving real soon. But it's a whole world of water and light out here on Route 1 stretching as far as the eye can see in front of us, behind us, on every side, and Willie seems very far away all of a sudden like he's in the past already. Suddenly I remember Be Here Now is the name of that hippie smoke store on Duval. And here I am now with this crazy old man, driving up this narrow highway across the shining ocean. Names and signs flash past us: Summerland Key, Big Torch Key, which is the Key Deer habitat, the marker has a picture of the tiny deer with huge eyes just like those pictures of poor children in Mexico or someplace, my head gets kind of jumbled up sometimes but I have seen these pictures, maybe Paula showed us. We pass dive shops and RV parks and the Dolphin Research Center and a sign for the Bahia Honda State Park and then we're on the Seven Mile Bridge, "The biggest stretch of open water in the Keys," Mister Atlas announces.

"Oh gosh," I say but I can hardly speak, for we are driving through the air now across the water, which spreads out pale and shiny on either side of us, to the farthest edge of the world. This lasts forever and then we are in Marathon suddenly, which is a real town with businesses and restaurants and fancy vacation houses and real hotels. We have to slow down in all the traffic, and now there are plenty of places to turn around.

Mister Atlas looks over at me. "I know, I know," he says. "I gotta take you back."

"But can't we stop for some food first?" Now I'm getting real hungry, and my baby is real hungry, too. Something comes over his face then, all of a sudden, stuck in traffic in Marathon. "Honey, I'll tell you what," he says, "I'm going to turn around soon and drive you back to Key West, but lemme take you out for a nice lunch first. Right up the road here is Susan's favorite restaurant, we used to stop there every time we drove up the Keys, sometimes we'd just come up here for a day trip, for lunch. We used to come up here all the time. So let me take you out to lunch, honey, and then I'll take you home."

I hold up my hand to look at Miss Susan's bracelet, turning my wrist in the sunshine so that every charm on it starts twinkling. Home? I'm thinking, for I don't really have one. I'm just along for the ride. "Well, sure," I say, settling back in the seat. "That sounds real nice."

I get tickled at all the crazy stuff we're driving past, a motel named the Last Resort and Crazy Billy's Country Store and a big billboard saying "Your Wife Is Hot, Better Get Your AC Fixed!" and a whole lot of manatee statues holding people's mailboxes in their mouths, they are real popular around Marathon. One sign says GATOR HEADS AND WIND CHIMES. Everything is so crazy in the Keys, and people will do anything, which frees you up some, I guess, and might be why it's so popular. Anyhow I'm feeling real good—but real hungry— by the time Mister Atlas turns into SID AND ROXY'S GREEN TURTLE INN, SINCE 1947 in Islamorada, a name I just love to say over and over, "Islamorada, Islamorada." You don't say the S, it's like island. Islamorada.

Maybe I'll name my baby Islamorada, now that would be a beautiful name for a girl.

The Right Thing

3:15 pm. The pink cab stops directly in front of the pink trailer, which appears to be absolutely closed up, empty, uninhabited. No bike, no car, no nothing. Willie knows this is the place, though he has never been here, she wouldn't let him come. "Wait here, please," Willie tells the cabbie, who says something in his own language. "Just keep the meter running," Willie says. He uncoils himself to get out and walk up to the grimy door. He is dressed for the airport—jeans, the red tennis shoes, but a clean white shirt and a wrinkled seersucker sports coat and the Red Sox cap. He's going back to where he belongs, to be the person he's supposed to be. He holds the envelope in his hand. Looks like he's missed her, her and her friend Tamika both. Friend girls. His hair falls in his eyes as he shakes his head. He doesn't feel good about any of this, but what else is he supposed to do? His plane leaves in an hour, first to Miami, then the change for Boston.

He steps up on the cinderblock, then knocks, then knocks

again, then almost falls backward off the cinderblock when the door opens abruptly revealing a stocky, heavily tattooed young man wearing cutoffs and nothing else.

"Yeah?" the guy tosses his head, drops of water flying out around him in a kind of halo in the sun. "You looking for somebody?"

For a minute Willie doesn't know what he should do, if he should say her name or not. He doesn't know who the guy is.

Then the guy cocks his head, narrows his eyes. "Wait a minute. Wait a minute. I got it. So you got something for Dee Dee there? Okay dude. I'll make sure she gets it, don't worry. She's out right now, she's gotta job, you know, yeah they've both got jobs, both my girls. Okay then. Thanks, I'll give it to her."

Just like that he takes the envelope and shuts the metal door in Willie's face. For a minute Willie stands there, but what can he do? He's never had an actual address for her, he doesn't even know the address here, and doesn't see it posted anyplace. It's enough money, though. It's all he can do. Too late, he wonders if she'll ever see it. He slams his fist into the side of the trailer, then retraces his steps to the waiting cab, rubbing his knuckles. He takes one more long look at the trailer before it's gone, then he sees it in the rearview mirror, then it's gone completely, just gone.

Green Turtle Inn

~~~~~~~~~~~~~~~~~~~~~~~~

Mister Atlas did not tell me that the Green Turtle Inn would be such a big deal, very historic and lots of people, so I've got to do some fast work to get ready before I can even think of walking in there. Luckily I've got all my makeup in my bag, but I mess up the eyeliner big-time when he parks with a bump and a screech in the enormous lot.

"Come on, come on, you don't need all that shit," he's saying, but then it takes him a real long time to get himself up and out of the car, and so I get my face fixed after all. I know I should never be wearing cutoffs into such a place as this! But then I get out and I can't find him. And then sure enough, there he is peeing against the wheel of a white Cadillac!

"Sometime you're gonna get caught," I warn him, but he just grins and pulls up his sweatpants.

He takes my arm like I am a Princess for real, and we make our way across the huge parking lot together. The

Green Turtle Inn is the strangest-looking place you can ever imagine, lots of really old green wooden buildings all jammed together, plus some kind of old hotel out back, they're not even trying to look fancy! They want to look old! I'm feeling a little bit better about my cutoffs by the time Mister Atlas pushes the big door open and then all of a sudden we are in another world, like an old James Bond movie. We used to watch a lot of old movies at the program, and you can learn a lot from them, believe it or not.

So the Green Turtle Inn is all red leather and dark wood and a long long bar with a big mirror and really fancy old-fashioned lamps with colored glass shades hanging everyplace, and bartenders and waiters in black and white. The walls are covered with pictures of famous people including President Nixon and Marilyn Monroe and a lot of people I don't know the names of. Mister Atlas drags me along, turning back to say, "That's Dean Martin singing 'Little Old Wine Drinker Me'" over the sound system. But the Green Turtle Inn is packed with people not any more dressed up than I am, so I start feeling better. Pretty good. Then real good. The Green Turtle Inn is sophisticated and unprecedented (words). A silver-haired waiter shows us to a red leather booth.

"So," Mister Atlas says, leaning across the white tablecloth, "you ready to eat some green turtle soup?"

"NO!" I practically scream, then he laughs and says, "Okay, hon, there's plenty of other things on the menu," which turns out to be really big and heavy in its red leather folder. Mister Atlas explains that the Green Turtle Inn has been around since 1947 when turtle steaks were really popular. *Yuck*, I'm thinking. He says they also had a cannery across the street where they once processed more than a thousand pounds of turtle meat every week. "Really?" I say. "That much?" and he says, "Oh yeah, honey, it was real popular before the government got in the act. Now it's against the law to kill them and sell them, hell that was a big business in Key West, they used to bring the turtles in on boats and then keep them in these big pens in the water called the Turtle Kraals. Real close to where Susan had her gallery."

"Ahem!" says the gorgeous waiter who is probably gay or maybe he is actually a she, who knows? Who knows anything? Anyhow this waiter has great cheekbones.

Mister Atlas orders a piña colada for himself and a glass of pinot grigio for me. "I'm not supposed to drink," I say immediately, but he just says, "Oh come on, nobody's supposed to drink! But we gotta have a toast!" and nods to the waiter and says, "Bring us some water, too."

"Have you got any chips?" I ask and the waiter smiles and nods and brings a whole bowl of tortilla chips and some hummus and nuts, too, along with our drinks. Just one drink isn't going to hurt my little Islamorada, I know, so I lean back against the red leather and enjoy it, nibbling a chip with hummus. I could get used to this! For lunch I have a fish sandwich with fries and coleslaw because I know I have got to eat my vegetables, too, and Mister Atlas has a big cheeseburger and fries, which I know darn well he is not supposed to eat. He is going to die before I ever get him back to Key West and then everybody's going to be so mad at us. I try to think about Miss Pat and Miss Maribeth and how mad they'll be, but it doesn't seem to matter so much right now, and it doesn't matter at all with my second glass of pinot grigio.

"That's a girl!" Mister Atlas says.

A lady bartender at the bar keeps looking at me and when I get up to go to the bathroom she follows me down the little hall and says, "Honey, are you okay? Are you here of your own free will?" and I give her a big smile and say, "Yes ma'am, I'm with my grandfather."

And then when I'm eating my five-inch-high key lime pie, Mister Atlas leans across the table and says, "So okay, honey, when's the wedding? You gonna invite me?" He's smiling a big smile.

And I reckon I can't help it all of a sudden, I start crying into my napkin, the biggest, whitest, nicest napkin in the whole world. Dammit Dee Dee, I'm thinking even as I do this, goddamn you!

"Wait a minute, wait a minute here. I just asked you a simple question. When's the wedding?"

And I just keep on crying, I can't stop.

"So." Mister Atlas leans forward in the booth and makes his hands into a little tent and looks at me across it. "So maybe there's not going to be any wedding after all, huh. Is that what you're telling me? This guy's not gonna marry you? He's running out on you?"

I put my napkin over my face and keep on crying and it's all dark in there under the napkin, just like being in the back of that panel truck. Maybe I knew this all along but I never really believed it before right now, this minute in the Green Turtle Inn. But you know what? It's okay.

"It's okay," I tell Mister Atlas. "He is just a boy."

"Huh." Mister Atlas is still leaning forward, looking serious. "So whaddya gonna do, honey?"

I take my napkin off. "I'm going to have my baby, and I'm going to take the best care of her in the world."

"Well, honey, that's a damn tall order," Mister Atlas says, "but I'll tell you something. I may be a dying man, but I'm a *rich* dying man, and I can still do what I want, and I'm going to help you out with this, whatever you want to do. I'm going to help you out because you're a fine girl, and you took good care of my Susan."

"Really?" is all I can think to say. This is the nicest thing I have ever heard of.

"Yeah really. My pleasure. No strings attached." He's smiling his old crooked smile. "We'll get you straightened out, whatever you want to do. What the fuck. But first we've gotta go home and face the music."

"No," I hear myself saying.

"No?" he repeats. "Well, whaddya wanna do then, for Pete's sake?"

"I want to go to Disney World." This just comes to me out of the blue, but it is absolutely true. "I've always wanted to go to Disney World, all my life. In fact it is the opposite of my life. I want to see the Magic Kingdom. I want to see the Princesses. I never got to go to Disney World when I was a girl, and now I'm going to be a mother but I want to see the Magic Kingdom first. Just something for me, because when my baby comes it will be all about her, and then I will take such good care of her, Mister Atlas. I will."

Mister Atlas raises both hands up in the air. "I give up," he says.

"So how far is it from here?" I ask him.

He leans back in the comfy red booth. "Well, shit, it's just up the road in Orlando, only maybe three, four hours from here. We go on up to Disney, though, we gotta spend the night."

"Can we afford to do that?" I ask, and he starts laughing.

"Sure, we can afford to do that. It's small change, peanuts. We can afford to do any goddamn thing you want, what else am I gonna do? So yeah, and I won't even touch you. I swear! Scout's honor."

"Oh I know that, Mister Atlas," I tell him, which is true. All of a sudden I'm laughing and crying both. "Actually you are the sweetest old man in the world, you just try to hide it all the time."

Mister Atlas doesn't even wait for the check, he just puts some money down on the table and stands up. "Done, kid. We better get back on the road then."

They're playing Judy Garland's "Moon River" on the PA system as we leave, I love that song.

After he pees against the white Cadillac again, we get all settled down in the little porch car again and I feel great, just great, riding along with a full tummy and a happy baby and the shiny blue water on both sides of us, and the open road ahead.

Snaggletooth

So Herb and not-Renee are cruising north up Route 1 and she's laughing at something he says, she's always laughing, she thinks he's a comedian for Christ's sake, she puts her hand up to cover the snaggletooth.

"Hey hey," he says, "So what's up with the hand business?"

"What do you mean, Mr. Atlas?" She leans forward to look at him.

"I mean you're always covering up your mouth when you laugh. You've got a pretty mouth, damn it. Why do you do that?"

She looks surprised, eyes round. "Well, I don't know. I mean, do I do that?"

"Yeah. You do that, honey. All the time."

"I guess I'm embarrassed about my tooth. I mean I *am* embarrassed right now, if you want to know. I wish you'd quit talking about it." Now suddenly she looks real upset, both hands up to her face, and Herb realizes he has fucked up.

"Why? What's so embarrassing about it? Hey, I think it's real cute. It's like your trademark or something."

"Half of my tooth got broke off in an accident, if you want to know. And my arm got broke and I got all bruised up and my mouth got cut real bad, too. See? See here?" She leans over to show him the small scar at the side of her mouth. Of course it wasn't an accident, but she doesn't say.

Herb peers at her mouth and the Porsche veers over into the right lane and a car horn blasts at him and he blows his horn right back. You've gotta be assertive in this world. The meek don't get shit. "I can't see a thing, honey. You're a doll. You gotta know that. Be proud."

He sounds like Paula. So she risks something. She says, "No, look, if I could've gotten this tooth fixed I would have, believe me. I look at the pictures in the magazines. I know how girls are supposed to look. I'm going to get this tooth fixed sometime or maybe I'll get a whole new one."

"Wait a minute, wait a minute. You really wanna get your tooth fixed? I'll get that tooth fixed for you the minute we get back to Key West. I know this guy, this real good dentist down there, an orthodontist for Christ's sake, that's the ticket, Dr. Ferguson. No problem."

"Really? You would do that?"

"Yeah, really. But I'll tell you something. You look good like it is. It looks good to have one little thing wrong, I'm telling you. You don't wanna be perfect. Perfect might be pretty, but it's not beautiful." Herb can tell she doesn't get this, what the hell. He is thinking of Roxana as a girl, as a young woman, with that sweet gap between her front teeth.

She leans back and sighs. "That's okay, I guess it's just me."

"Hell no, I'm gonna do it, I'm telling you. Scout's honor." Like he was ever a fucking Boy Scout.

Dee Dee takes her hand down and gives him a big smile. "That's a girl!"

"But now I might take a little nap, okay? I'm getting kind of tired, all of a sudden." She balls up her pink sweatshirt and puts it against the door and then she's asleep. Just like that. Like a puppy or something. Mouth slightly open, snuffly breathing.

HERB LOOKS OUT the window at the Theater of the Sea where a shark killed somebody one time, or maybe somebody killed the shark, or he thinks they did. But in his mind's eye he is seeing Roxana, his own Roxana, who had that gap that he loved between her front teeth, it gave her the cutest smile, like a girl in a fairytale. Or Raggedy Ann, the Raggedy Ann dolls were big then. When Herb was looking for the keys to the Porsche, these keys he's using right now, he came across the little cardboard picture book they'd gotten made in the Photo Studio on the Midway at the Crystal Beach amusement park when he came back from the navy that first time, money in his pocket. They took the day trip from Buffalo to Ontario on the *Americana* steamer. Herb will never forget that day at Crystal Beach, riding the famous Cyclone so huge that you can't even believe it keeps climbing up and up and up, she was hugging his neck and closing her eyes, then screaming all the way down until she started laughing and couldn't stop. Herb didn't blame her, it scared the hell out of him, too. But she was dead game, Roxana, always. "Let's do it again, Herby," she said, and they did, and this time he kissed her all the way down, really planted one on her. They rode the Tilt-A-Whirl and the Wild Mouse. She was fearless, Roxana.

They were wobbly by the time they walked out to the boardwalk and saw all the people in the water and sitting and lying on the sandy beach in their bathing suits. Herb had learned to swim in the navy but Roxana didn't know how. They took off their shoes and walked out on the sand, far out to the water's edge, holding hands. He wished they had bathing suits because he wanted to see her white freckled skin and her whole self out in the sun like this. They sat down on the sand, surprised by how warm it was, running it through their fingers, they made little sand hills to cover up their feet. That warm sand on his feet felt so good and Herb felt so good, he felt better than he has ever felt since. After a while he got up and made a big heart in the flat, gray sand near the water's edge and wrote their initials in it, H.A.+ R.D., and then they walked back to the Midway with their arms around each other, looking at the sights.

"Let's go in," he'd said when they came to the Photo Studio, though she'd held back and said, "Oh Herby, it'll be too expensive." But he wanted it. He wanted some pictures of them together to take back with him on the ship, him in his uniform and her in her yellow flowered sundress, and so he asked for the special, six pictures in a hardcover book. "They'll be memories," the old man said, the photographer, rigging up different scenes, a tropical background and a city skyline and two fancy chairs and a little table like in a soda shop. He got them laughing and then posing in crazy hats and then smiling to beat the band and then kissing, really kissing like crazy when he told them to stand in front of the city skyline. Then the photographer came out from under the camera's black hood and said, "Okay, kids, that's great," but when Herb tried to pay him, he wouldn't take the money. He was crying, that old man. Herb's about to cry now, thinking about it. He's glad he looked in his old leather suitcase for his golf shoes. He's glad he found the little book, all soft around the edges from him holding it all through the war. "This is me and my girlfriend," he told his buddies in Korea. *"This is us."*

Tavernier

Tavernier is the last official sign Dee Dee sees before she leans back and gets comfortable. Tavernier, Tavernier . . . it's such a pretty word, maybe she'll name her baby Tavernier instead of Islamorada but then again maybe not. Islamorada is more feminine. The road runs ahead like a silver ribbon across the water, into the sky. "The road goes on forever but the party never ends," whose song is that? Robert Earle Keen. Mama didn't live long enough to know that one but it could have been her theme song and she could have sung it great, she could sing anything. Dee Dee pulls the brim of her sequined baseball cap down and closes her eyes. She's on the road again. She thinks back to the time she got away from Smiley when that one guy, really he was just a boy, named Edwin, showed up to get something for his daddy who was dying in terrible pain from cancer but the insurance had run out. Smiley pushed Edwin on her the way he always did. Edwin shook his head and blushed when Smiley did that, but the next time he came, two weeks later, he followed Dee Dee out onto the screen porch where he just sat real still and looked down at his feet. He had on these big clodhopper boots. The transistor radio was playing Trisha Yearwood.

"You don't have to do nothing," he said. "I just want to say something to you."

"Oh come on, honey," she said automatically.

"No, I'm serious," he said. "You're just a girl. You need to get out of here."

And the minute he said that, it was like something came over Dee Dee and she knew he was right. Edwin had soft blue eyes and thick glasses and curly brown hair and a UK cap.

"I'll tell you what," he said. "I'll be coming back over here again on Wednesday two weeks from now to get Daddy some more medicine. And you be ready, you hear?"

He never touched her, and Dee Dee never said a thing. She bit her lip and nodded.

Two weeks later, she had some clothes tied up in a satchel under the bed, and when Edwin showed up and got his daddy's pills, she led him back to the screen porch and he grabbed her satchel out from under the cot and they were gone. Edwin had borrowed his uncle's van and she crouched down in the front seat while he drove slow out of the hollow and then he floored it. Nobody followed them. Dee Dee will always remember how it felt, mile after mile, she sat up higher in the seat. Then she started laughing and he started laughing, too.

Dee Dee reached for him just out of habit but he said, "No, no thanks, honey, you can just save that for your husband."

"I ain't got a husband," she said. "I'm not but fourteen years old."

"Well, that's the point, ain't it?" he said. He said he was aiming to be a minister of God. His name was Edwin Applewhite, she would never forget it.

Then he asked her where she wanted to go and she said "Florida" right out of the blue. She said she wanted to go to a bus station, that she was going to stay with her sister in Tampa. She just made that up but she wished it was true. She had taken some of Smiley's money out of his safe box, and she was wondering if he knew that by now.

"All right," Edwin said, and then he drove her all the way to the bus station in Asheville and she got a ticket for Jacksonville, which was as close as she could get to Tampa on the money she had.

Dee Dee had gone to the back of the bus and gotten into her seat when she thought to look back as the bus was pulling out, and what did she see but Edwin Applewhite running beside the bus, waving his red hat like crazy and hollering something at her. She never did know what he was trying to say, but that picture of him stayed in her mind for years. What if she had stopped the bus and gotten off and gone home with him and become a minister's wife? Or something else? Anything, anything would have been better than what was going to happen to her next.

DEE DEE HAD to get off the bus in Jacksonville, it was the end of the line. All she had had to eat for the last eight hours was a package of Little Debbie oatmeal cookies, six of them, and two Mountain Dews. She had $38 left and it was starting to get really dark when she pushed the big glass door of the bus station open and looked out at the empty city square with the soldier statue in the middle and big trees blowing in the wind, for a storm was coming up. She didn't have a raincoat, or any coat, just the pink hoodie sweatshirt on her back and her satchel, a laundry bag with some clothes in it.

She stood on the sidewalk with the wind whipping trash around her feet and then a car pulled over to the curb and the good-looking young driver stuck his head out the window and said, "Hey honey, you need a ride?" Then the back window went down and a dark-haired girl said, "Come on! You can come with us." There was another man in the front seat, too, a little older. He poked his head around the driver's head. "You look tired, dear, come on," he said, and then the girl said, "It's okay, honey, we're going to eat," and so Dee Dee got in the car with a big sigh of relief. They started talking and drove through Jacksonville, past parks and palm trees.

And then they pulled into a Ruby Tuesday and the older guy, whose name was Gary, ordered beers and nachos for everybody and then they had a nice dinner. Dee Dee ordered the fried shrimp since she was in Florida.

Close up, Dee Dee could see that the other girl, Brenda, had what was left of a black eye under her makeup. By the time they got through eating, Dee Dee was so tired she was about to die. She didn't remember too much after they checked into a Motel 6 where the younger guy Brian gave them a little goodnight drink, he said it was a toddy, and the older guy said, "Don't worry, sugar, we're here for you." The next day they were selling the girls on the internet right out of that Motel 6 and that was just the start of it.

After two more days there, they took the girls on a shopping spree at Target, where Dee Dee bought some cute new tops and cutoffs, and then they drove them over to Atlantic Beach, where they started selling them out of a pretty classy Travelodge on the beach and after that a crummy Red Roof Inn at Jacksonville Beach.

That's when Brenda started crying and couldn't quit, so Gary took her back into the bathroom and did something to her that made her scream, which was muffled immediately, and then he came out and then the water was running and then when Brenda finally came out she looked okay, just pale, and she nodded at them, and that was it. Whatever he did to her was something you couldn't see. No more bruises.

Later that night, Brenda somehow got out of the room. When she asked the guy at the desk in the lobby of the Red Roof Inn for help, he called the police. The rest of them were still sound asleep when three cops came busting in and took them all to the police station.

That's when Dee Dee first heard about shelters, and the Family Crisis Service that tries to help you get a job, but by then she didn't want help or a job, she didn't think she could do a job, mostly she just wanted a drink and some fun, so it wasn't long before she was back in the life, which was always right out there waiting. This went on for a long time. Some guys pretended they really liked her and she always fell for that. One guy sold her to a drug dealer in exchange for his drugs, one guy took her to Gainesville and held her captive in an old shack out in a swamp, bringing other guys out there, until one of them knifed him and took her away, but then he turned out to be weird. This went on and on. Dee Dee got numb. She never thought about another life. She never thought she could have another life. The one thing she would never do is go back to North Carolina or anyplace where Smiley might be. So she kept moving south, away from Smiley, that was all she cared about, and then after a while she didn't care about anything and she was flat broke and real tired when she ran into Madame Lola in Tampa.

Madame Lola sold thirteen girls who worked for her along with a few other part-timers who she said were marriage therapists. Madame Lola sold Dee Dee for six months until she got busted. While Dee Dee was there, she slept on a toddler-sized mattress on the floor and did what the Madame told her to, even when deep down she wanted to object. She went to men's homes or apartments or motels six or seven times a day. Some of these jobs lasted a half hour, some an hour or more. Sometimes she spent the night. Sometimes they were family men, fathers and grandfathers. Some were nice. Some were not. Madame Lola lived in a green stucco house in an old, run-down part of Tampa. The madame herself slept in a big fancy bed in the living room, with one eye open, she always said. The girls who worked for her hung out in another room between jobs, talking, playing cards, watching TV. They all liked *Game of Thrones*, and one girl, Katrina, knew almost all the answers on *Jeopardy*. Carla and Brigitte liked to sing with Dee Dee. The room was full of the clothes they wore: miniskirts, high-heel shoes, fancy lingerie,

Dee Dee loved the clothes. She didn't get to know the other girls as well as well as she wanted to. They were all busy. Thinking back, Dee Dee doesn't know what to say. It was a life, and she didn't think she deserved any other life.

Dee Dee was asleep the night when Madame Lola got busted, it was like an army of cops all around the house, shining big flashlights everywhere so nobody could get away. The girls had to grab what they could and walk out into the flashing lights with their arms up. Madame wore her fur coat and waved at everybody, and one girl, Suzy, shimmied up the walk to the vans. They took everybody in.

As it turned out, that was the best thing that ever happened to Dee Dee.

Key Largo

~~~~~~~~~~~~~~~~~~~~~~~~~~~~~~~~~~~

The girl is still sleeping like a baby when he has to hit the brakes around MM 92, a few miles before Buttonwood Sound, son of a bitch. What is all this goddamn construction all of a sudden? If Herb was running this highway system, he'd have them doing this construction in the dead of summer when there's not so much traffic or tourists, son of a bitch!

Dee Dee jerks awake, sits up, stretches, smiles. Like a kid. Just like a little kid. "Hi," she says. "I had a nap. What's going on?"

"Goddamn construction," he says. "Look at all these goddamn orange cones. I tell you what, honey. The wealthiest person in America is the man that makes all these goddamn orange cones. These barricade things for the highways. I'm not kidding you. Look at 'em." Herb takes one hand off the wheel and points ahead. "Mile after mile. Hundreds of orange cones. Thousands of orange cones. Millions of orange cones, all over America." The car swerves.

"Oh, Mister Atlas, watch out!" But she's giggling now.

"I'm not shitting you, sweetie. It's a damn gold mine."

"Wonder where they keep them, though?" she asks. "I mean, when they're not using them? All the cones. They must have the biggest warehouse in the world."

"You got it, baby. A great big warehouse on Easy Street."

"Oh, Mister Atlas!" She's still laughing but Herb is serious.

"It's some kind of con job, you can bet your sweet ass. Only one or two guys make all the money in America, anyway. Sam Walton and Jeff Bezos and all those computer kids in the T-shirts. You've just gotta be creative. Very creative. But orange cones, who knew? And it's a damn good question, where do they keep 'em? Probably out in the desert someplace, like where they make bombs and shoot up rockets. We the American people, the so-called American people, don't know nothing about what goes on in the desert. We don't know shit about the desert."

Herb eases over to the right to avoid a truck pulling a house down the middle of the road. A house! Got that? On this crazy little road? But at least the girl seems to be enjoying the drive, laughing at a billboard that says PSYCHIC OIL CHANGE AND GAS. They've gotta lot of these crazy combination joints down here for sure, crazy combos, yeah, like a dying geezer and a pregnant girl. Herb is not totally crazy though, he's just pissed off. And there's a lot of stuff to be pissed off about in this goddamn world. And speaking of piss, he makes a quick right into the psychic gas station, switches off the ignition, and asks her to pump the gas while he heads for the restroom.

Dee Dee is delighted to do this. She likes to be useful. And pumping gas is a thing she learned to do at Rainbow Farm, in Life Skills, along with driving. After, she puts Herb's credit card carefully into the little zipped section of her purse before going to the bathroom herself, not a fun experience! She washes her hands and waves them vigorously, throwing off silver drops in the sunshine as she trots back to the little yellow car.

Before he can pull back out into the heavy traffic on Route 1 North, Herb has to idle for a long time in front of the rundown Thrifty Plaza, which consists of the Lion's Den Adult Superstore behind a dark shade, Carla's Cuban Café, and one of those trendy churches that takes up the last three storefronts. "BE HERE NOW! A Cool Congregation!" says the rainbow sign. Herb waits impatiently.

"Shit, this is taking forever," he says. "We coulda gone into Carla's here and gotten a Cuban and eaten it by now."

At this her stomach growls—she's hungry again. But then she's hungry most of the time.

"Didja ever go to church?" Herb asks the girl, just making talk, but she seems to take this question very seriously, wrinkling up her pretty forehead, thinking back.

"Sometimes when I was real little," she says after a pause, "up in the mountains. I remember the singing. We went to some open-air revivals and singings, too."

Herb doesn't have a clue what she's talking about, but he looks over at her seriously. "So, like, what did you sing?" and to his amazement she bursts out into, "Amazing Grace, how sweet the sound, that saved a wretch like me. I once was lost, but now am found, was blind, but now I see." Her last perfect wavering note hangs in the air.

"God damn, honey, that's beautiful," he says. "So, you went to that church, then? You and your family?"

Now she blushes, looks down. "No, not really," she says. "I wish we had of, though."

"Why's that?" He's trying to look at her face, but she keeps it turned away, looking out the window at the endless freak parade along Route 1.

"Oh I don't know, maybe I would have been a better person if I had," she says. Then, after a long pause, "It's very hard to be a good person."

"Shit, baby," Herb says, as the traffic starts to move again, "it's hard to be any kind of a person," at which she laughs, unexpectedly. There's a lot going on in that pretty little head, Herb is realizing.

And now finally, heading up the long, sweet stretch to Key Largo, traffic thins out and so do the damn orange cones, in fact they disappear around MM 100. Silver water stretches out like heaven on either side of the car. Herb thinks about putting the top down but then realizes he's forgotten how to do it, so what? He pushes the buttons and rolls all the windows down instead.

"Mister Atlas! You're messing up my hair!" Dee Dee squeals, yelling over the wind, but it's a mock complaint, she's loving it, too, he can tell, her platinum-blond hair streaming out behind her.

"I guess I'm too old to have that problem," he yells back.

She smiles. She's been trimming his hair for him, whatever's still left to cut, as she has been doing Pat's and Maribeth's hair, too. "You're never too old to have that problem. Your hair is still growing, you know. Hair never stops growing. It grows even after death."

"Ha! Maybe I'm already dead, then! That would solve a lot!" Herb is cracking himself up again.

"That is just ludicrous!" Dee Dee announces, trying out the new word on him. She's having so much fun, she knows it's just crazy but suddenly she can feel her baby move, she thinks—maybe she's having fun, too! Dee Dee thinks about Flamingo and Margarita for names.

They pass the fancy entrance to John Pennecamp Coral Reef State Park on the right, at MM102.5. Herb jerks a thumb at it. "America's first underwater state park," he says. "They gotta big statue of Jesus Christ down there in the water some-place, for all the fish and dead people to look at."

"They do not!"

"No shit. If you'd brought your bathing suit, you could dive down there and see him."

"Oh, Mister Atlas, don't you know I can't swim?" she says, but suddenly she thinks she'd like to learn. Travel is certainly educational, broadening. A deep calm comes over Dee Dee then, driving up Key Largo, the long, straight road ahead divided now by a blue concrete wall, the big blue sky above, the shining water as far as the eye can see on either side of them, and all those little islands, wonder if anybody lives on them? Surely some people do, and Dee Dee thinks she would like to, in a little house with her baby. She also likes the name Largo, though Largo sounds more like a boy's name, and her baby is definitely not a boy. She settles back in her seat.

"Okay, honey, look up," he's saying, "I know you wanna see this."

"What?" she takes off her sunglasses and the world is a blaze of light and color and people, so many people all of a sudden. They're in a real town now.

"This is Key Largo," Mr. Atlas says like he's making an announcement, like it's a big deal or something.

She looks at him, waiting.

"Key Largo, get it? Humphrey Bogart? The movie? 'Here's looking at you, kid?'"

Dee Dee just stares at him. Without her sunglasses, her eyes are very wide and very blue, the eyes of a child. Fuck, she *is* a child.

"Okay. So you never heard of it, right?"

She puts her hand up to her mouth, smiling. "Yes sir," she says. "That's right."

"Well you watch it sometime. It's a classic." Nobody knows what I know, he's thinking, and nobody gives a fuck. About any of it.

"Could we please stop and get some ice cream?" she asks. "Or maybe some frozen custard? Look, there's a place."

Sighing, Herb pulls into the lot with the polka-dot building and the giant rotating ice-cream cone on top of it. With difficulty he gets himself out from under the wheel and stands up slowly and heads off to pee while Dee Dee takes her place in the long line. But when he comes back, he's too tired to stand in the damn line in the sun.

"Here, honey." He opens up the money belt and hands Dee Dee a bill before he staggers back to the car and collapses into the seat.

"Mister Atlas, you know I can't use that. They won't have change. Here, wait, I've got it, don't worry." She digs deep in the sparkling purse and comes up waving a twenty, then calls back to ask, "What kind do you want?" and when he doesn't seem to get that, she calls again, "What flavor of ice cream, Mister Atlas?"

"Anything, honey, I don't give a damn." He wishes she wouldn't have yelled his name out like that. He leans back against the hot seat, closing his eyes, remembering all the times he had brought Susan up the Keys. They stayed in that classy place she liked, what the hell was it? Oh yeah, the Cheeca Lodge, low key but elegant, like Susan herself. Martinis, massages. He's thinking of Susan's long white legs so it's a big jolt when the kid comes back with his ice cream. Mint chocolate chip, his favorite. How'd she know? And why is that crew cut guy staring at them as Herb pulls out? Just standing there by his car, damn little Prius, looking at them. Well, the girl, she attracts attention. Or maybe the guy just likes the car, his beautiful yellow Porsche. Probably that's all. But still.

Rainbow Farm

We're driving north on the Sunshine Parkway around Miami, which is nothing but big buildings going on and on forever and houses that all look alike set two feet apart and then the biggest IKEA in the world and then more houses, when all of a sudden I see a road going off to the left and a sign for Belle Glade, Florida, and I almost jump out of my seat. That's not so far from Rainbow Farm, where Paula saved my life.

But first I had to go to prison, where I was safe for the first time in a long time, maybe for the first time in my life, and by then I was just so tired, real tired, and I knew I had a drinking problem and a drug problem to get over with, and I knew I couldn't do it by myself. I was pretty sick, too, I had herpes and gonorrhea and I was real anemic, it turned out. I weighed a hundred pounds. I didn't have any family to write down on that paper in the blank that said Family, or any friends to put in the blank that said Friends. Your friends are not your friends when you get in the shape I was in. I knew I wouldn't stay straight a day on the street, I'd just go back to it all, because I was good at it. That's what you do, isn't it? You do what you know. What you're good at. I wanted to die, or I thought I did. But I didn't die. They put me on antibiotics and gave us real food not bar food or snack stuff and in spite of myself I started getting better.

They gave us a real Christmas dinner on Christmas Day, turkey and dressing and gravy and green bean casserole and pumpkin pie, which I had never even tasted before. I ate every bite of it. They gave us each a red-and-green basket with a bow on it, a gift from Walgreens with soap and lipstick and lotion and a toothbrush and a little thing of toothpaste and shampoo and candy in it, Hershey kisses. I looked out the window through the bars and the sun was shining on the big leaves of a palm tree, which had a little monkey sitting up there on the coconuts, it scared me to death and I screamed and then everybody else ran over to the window to look at him, too, and it was like he was playing with us, making faces and scratching his little belly, and we all started laughing. We were just girls mostly.

Then Mrs. Johnson, the big Black lady with a long scar running down her beautiful face, said "Okay girls, now settle down, we've got a special Christmas gift for you," and that was how we got to watch Dolly Parton's Christmas show on the television, they had taped it for us to see. I have always loved Dolly Parton! She had on this gorgeous white sequin outfit and she looked so beautiful, like a Christmas angel herself. I knew she had had a hard life and she came from the mountains, too, just like me. I started thinking about Christmases back home when I was real little and we made popcorn strings for the tree with a needle and thread and the popcorn, and sang the old carols in front of the tree. "Away in a Manger," "The Cherry Tree Carol," "What Child Is This?" . . . and then I thought, well they are all dead now but I'm *not!* Dee Dee, I said to myself, you have got to get yourself together. You've got to do something.

And then I started feeling better, and so when the TV special was over, I started singing right there in the day room and then some of those other girls joined in on "Jingle Bells" and "We Wish You a Merry Christmas" and especially "Santa Claus Is Coming to Town," I was going for the peppy songs. I say girls but some of them were old, thirties even forties. Some of them looked like hell, too burned out to make it, and I knew they wouldn't. They scared me to death because I knew they had been girls one time, just like me.

So about a week later when Mrs. Johnson said she was recommending me for this sex-victim recovery program called Rainbow Farm, I signed right there on the line. Deirdre June Mullins, I wrote. I'm your girl! I said. Because what did I have to lose? For one thing, it would get me out of prison. And for another thing, they would teach you a trade for the future. I was sort of thinking that singing would be my trade, or maybe cocktail waitress, but then they said that those would not be a reliable living and it might be a dangerous lifestyle so I could choose between nails or practical nurse or vet tech so I picked nails because I thought it would be the easiest to get a job, and also I have always loved nails. They say you should always do what you love.

THE PROGRAM ITSELF was somewhere outside of Belle Glade, in the middle of no place. They took three of us there in a van straight out of prison, me and a blonde named Candy who used to be real pretty, you could tell, only now she wouldn't look at anybody, she just looked down, and a big, tough red-headed woman named Sam who had one arm in a cast. My heart started thumping so hard when we turned off of the interstate onto State Road 27 and started driving back into the mangrove swamps down a road that got littler and littler. It was rough out there. This was my first time ever in the back country of Florida, and I was terrified.

"Looky there," said the prison guard that was driv-ing, Mister Butler, pointing at an old tree laying in the coffee-colored canal running alongside the road, and when I looked, that tree started moving and it was a big old crocodile!

"Just in case you was thinking about running away," Mister Butler said. He was laughing, "Hee, hee, hee."

We went deeper and deeper into the swamp until we came to a high chain-link fence and then a fancy iron gate with some kind of a shield on it, and then we went down a long straight drive up a low hill to a great big old white house that had once been a fine place, you could tell. I mean *Gone with the Wind*. Outbuildings in the back. The house had columns all across the front and a tall front door with a Christmas wreath on it. Red bow.

"That's where we're going?" It was the first thing Sam had said. "I'll be goddamned!" and we all laughed but then Mrs. Poindexter, the social worker lady in the front seat with Mister Butler, cleared her throat and said, "This is a real opportunity for you girls and don't you forget it. It's up to you to make the most of it."

"Yeah right. Fuck you," Sam said, under her breath so they couldn't hear it.

While we were still coming up the driveway, the front door opened and a tall woman came out and stood on the porch wearing a long skirt like a pioneer, just like somebody in *Little House on the Prairie*, one of my favorite books, and she looked strong enough to withstand anything such as outlaws or Indians or tornados. Mister Butler drove our van up to the house around the circle driveway, stopping in front of the porch, which we would learn to call the portico.

"Okay," Mrs. Poindexter said. "This is it. Get your things. You're going to get out now," and we got out and stood in a row to face the woman in the long skirt, waiting for us. The wind blew her skirt. It was real cold out there.

"Oh my darlings," she said, holding her arms out to us, "I know you have come a long way, a very long way, to be with us here at Rainbow Farm. You have had a hard, hard time. But you are safe here. You are safe. Everybody deserves a chance at a future, and this is yours. Welcome."

This was Paula. She stood there holding her arms out to us in the last rays of the clear December sun, and then she turned and opened the door. "Come," she said. "Come in, come in," and we went forward, Candy and me right up next to each other. It was scary. Important. I had a white plastic purse and an old yellow coat that the charity ladies had given me in prison, and a paper sack with a few more clothes in it, and that was all. Nothing. That's what I had. That's what I was. Nothing.

"You're home," Paula said. "You're safe." Then she shook hands with each one of us in turn. I don't think I had ever seen a woman shake hands with another woman before. It was like a little ceremony. I was the last one so I was real nervous when she got to me. She took my hand and held it tight, looking straight into my eyes, smiling. She had wide gray eyes and no makeup and long gray hair, pulled back. "Rainbow Farm was started by a lady who believed in you, and she left this whole place to you when she died. Welcome." I guess Paula might have already been sick by then, but maybe she didn't know it yet, and we for sure didn't know it.

I had my own little room up on the third floor, the first time I ever had a room to myself in my life. The ceiling was peaked because of the roof. The pink flowered wallpaper was peeling, but still nice. A little dresser and a single bed with a pink-and-green quilt that some person had actually made, you could see the needle marks and sometimes a mistake. A wooden table with a white milk glass lamp and a white Bible on it with the name Eugenia Williamson printed in gold. Who was she? I wondered if she was grown up or dead now. My skinny window looked out on the driveway we had come up, and there was an iron mesh screen beyond the glass.

My first night at Rainbow Farm I was so tired I didn't even take my clothes off but slept like the dead, but then the second

182 · LEE SMITH

night I got nervous and couldn't sleep a wink so I got up and went down one floor and that's when I met the first other girl I really talked to, Tamika, who couldn't sleep either and was sneaking a smoke out on the fire escape landing. "Hey girl," she said, handing me a cigarette. Tamika had a big grin and that sparkle in her eyes even then. Mischievous is the word. "Hey," I said. I had to smile back, lighting up, and then it was fine. Though I would come to like some of the other girls, too—there were twelve of us—Tamika became the first girl-friend I ever had, or friend girl, that's what Tamika called it.

Rainbow Farm was not really a farm at all but a place for us to stay and learn how to do things like balance a checkbook or boil an egg or use birth control or get a Social Security card or drive a car or take care of a baby or even read and write. One real sweet lady came in to teach what they called literacy classes, and later on she would get me to help her. We had nutrition and health classes, too, and self-esteem and self-protection. We all did okay except for Sam, who kept starting fights and got sent back to prison, and Gina, a girl from New Orleans who went away in an ambulance in the middle of the night after she cut her wrists in the bathtub on the second floor. After three months the rest of us got to go into town for the training school classes where we were just like anybody else, and after a while even Candy would look at you. Candy took Nurse Tech. Tamika took Business, where she learned how to use a cash register and wait on people, she could sell anybody anything. The teacher said Tamika's smile was her biggest asset. Beauty 101 is where I learned that I have a natural talent for nails as well as talking to people, such as always asking them about themselves. The teacher said I have a nice manner, too.

Different girls left Rainbow Farm at different times but Candy and Tamika and me stayed on as long as we could, helping with the new girls and such, until Candy got a nursing job in Ocala, where her sister lived. Then Paula got real sick and had to quit, and the new director's husband started hitting on Tamika, but the new director, Mrs. Kemp, wouldn't believe Tamika when she tried to tell her what he was doing, and then Mrs. Kemp accused Tamika and me of stealing from the office, which we did not. Mr. and Mrs. Kemp signed papers on us. It all got real bad real fast so Tamika and me just booked, hopping in that truck that one day in town, and ended up in Key West.

Trailer Park

~~~~~~~~~~

1:10 pm. Ricky glides into the trailer park, stopping under the big lignum vitae tree close to the highway, where he rolls up the windows, locks the car, and pockets the key before strolling over to the pink trailer, which is not looking so good these days, he notes. No plants in pots like that Airstream, no nice furniture, no awning, no barbecue grill. Nothing except some paper trash and one green plastic chair and one old white tennis shoe and an aluminum pie pan by the door—somebody feeding a cat? Not likely. He kicks at the tennis shoe, looks around. Motorcycle tracks in the dirt. Sure. A hog. The guy would have a hog. Car tracks, too, over at the side. Cars, pickups—who knows what's in that thick vegetation behind the trailer park, it's a real jungle, extending all the way over to the old Kmart parking lot. People probably living back in there, too.

Close up, the trailer is nasty, its pink paint covered by layers of dirt and mold. It must have been *real* pink to start out with, which would have been when? The eighties maybe? The seventies? Earlier? Shades are pulled down behind the nasty little windows like closed eyes. Ricky walks over to the door, steps up on the cinder block, knocks sharply. Knocks again. He couldn't say why, but something makes him think somebody's home. He waits, then raps again on the door. Out of the corner of his eye, he sees the closest shade move.

He steps back just a fraction, so she can see him. Then knocks again.

"Miss Torain," he says loudly. "Tamika? Ricky Estevez here, I need to talk to you for just a minute about your friend Dee Dee Mullins."

The door opens just a crack. "She's not here." A low, pretty voice.

"I'm sorry to hear that, honey. This makes my job a lot harder."

"What is your job, mister?" The door inches open.

Ricky sees a pretty, dark eye beneath the frizz of hair. "I'm looking for Mr. Herbert Atlas, who used to be Dee Dee's boss. I'm his stepson, Ricky."

A nod. Hair bobs in the crack of the door. "So what's the problem?"

"Apparently Dee Dee came over to see him at his home on Washington Street this morning, probably to tell him goodbye before he goes to a nursing home up in Del Ray. Several people saw her on the sidewalk, and in the yard. But it's moving day, so a lot's going on over there today, and somehow in all the confusion, Dee Dee and Mister Atlas disappeared."

"You shitting me." Now she opens the door, a pretty girl,

but wasted-looking. Ashy skin. Probably drugs. Gray sweat-pants and a pink T-shirt that says *Grrrl Power* on it, sad.

"No ma'am, I'm sorry to say. Apparently Mister Atlas somehow got hold of the keys to his Porsche Carrera, which he's not allowed to drive anymore, and took off in it, with Dee Dee in the car. This was several hours ago. I thought he might have given her a ride home, but you're telling me she's not here. "

"I'm telling you Dee Dee doesn't stay here anymore," Tamika says. "She's got a rich boyfriend now. So she stays over there, most of the time. If she was here, she'd be in that little green camper down on the end there. She pays Tony for it now. But she's not hardly ever here, I'm telling you."

"I guess I need to take a look at it, though." Ricky doesn't mention that he's already been by the house off Poor House Lane, where he knocked on the locked blue door repeatedly. Nobody was around except an old Asian guy doing exercises on the front porch who shook his head and shrugged when asked the whereabouts of William Farnsworth.

"Well, you go on down there then. She's not in there though."

Ricky nods and turns on his heel in the dirt.

"Hey mister," she calls out to him. "Who are you, any-how? You the police?"

"Family." Ricky tips his hat. "I told you." He feels eyes on him as he walks down the short line of trailers and campers, but nobody else comes outside. Probably some of them have got good reason to keep out of sight.

The small green camper is a piece of trash, but sort of

sweet, like a child's playhouse. Well shit, she's just a kid. The door has a new padlock on it, he sees. Cheap. Anybody could break it in a minute if they wanted to, but why bother? This is sad. And clearly she's not here. He could see her if she was, just by looking in the window. The tiny interior is neat as a pin—a folding bed, folded up into the wall, one small chair, a plastic plate and a cup on the little table, a child's cup and plate in fact, with Cinderella on it. Out of nowhere, Ricky remembers Dee Dee singing "Somewhere Over the Rainbow" to Susan. Susan loved it when she sang that. Three laundry baskets appear to contain everything Dee Dee owns: cosmetics, clothes, and the cases containing her beauty supplies. Ricky recognizes a pink tunic, a sparkly hat. She loves sparkles, this girl.

Ricky walks back past the closed trailers to the pink one, where Tamika's waiting for him now, sitting outside in the green plastic chair, knees crossed, swinging one long bare leg. It's clear that she used to be a very good-looking girl.

"So," she says.

"Nobody home," Ricky acknowledges. And nobody could ever actually *live* there, either. No running water. Chemical toilet. Electricity? For the first time he starts thinking of this girl as really damaged, as a damaged child herself. This changes things.

"So," Tamika says.

Ricky lights a cigarette for himself and one for Tamika and gives it to her. "Now let me ask you something else."

"Be my guest," she says. "I ain't got nothing else to do right now."

So is she coming on to him? Or is this just habit, an old habit? By now he's put together some idea of what these girls have been through. Not pretty.

"So here's the situation." He sits down on the cinder block. "Maybe you can help me out. It looks like Mr. Atlas drove away from his home on Washington Street sometime this morning, say, ten thirty, with your girlfriend in the car, and they're still gone. So what I need to know is, do you have any idea where they might be? Any idea at all? Any friends in town that she might want to visit? Any favorite place, a bar or a restaurant or anyplace else you can think of? Maybe some-place out at the beach? Does she like the beach?"

A big grin spreads over Tamika's face.

"Well?"

Tamika starts laughing. "Well first off, her and me, we ain't got no friends. We're friend girls, that's all. Just the two of us. Second thing, and I know this is going to sound crazy, but if she's not out at that boy's house, then the only place I can think of is Disney World. Yeah," she says at the look on his face. "I mean the Magic Kingdom, the real one, in Orlando. We used to talk all the time about going to Disney World, you know, to see the Princesses. We had this big thing about the Princesses. We knew all the songs from all those Princess movies, I mean Ariel and Belle and Tiana and all of them. The whole gang. We used to sing the songs from the movies, you know Dee Dee's a real good singer."

"I know," Ricky says.

"But Orlando's a long way away, isn't it? So I guess you think that's pretty crazy."

"Well, it's a crazy world." Ricky stomps out his cigarette, stands up, tips his hat to her. "Why don't you start taking better care of yourself, honey?"

"Well, maybe I will." Tamika squints up at him, smiles, then watches as he walks over to the big tree where the red car is. She really likes the car. She likes Ricky, too. She watches him get in, back up, and then step on it, taking off. She would have made a move on him if it wasn't for Jamal being so sick.

"Goddamnit, get back in here," Tony says through a crack in the door.

She wouldn't go back in there at all if she had some money, or a car, or anything. But she will, one day. She *will*. And she will have a job like she learned at Rainbow Farm. So she sighs, stretches, takes her time. She's barely inside when he slams her up against the door frame.

"You coming on to him, bitch. I heard that."

"No, Tony, I—"

"Yeah you were. And Disney World, huh? What are you, stupid? You coulda got some real money for that."

Silver Alert

~~~~~~~~~~~~~~~~~~~~~~~~

So yeah, all right, they're just cruising along at 72 miles per hour on the Don Shula Expressway going around Miami—Don Shula, that's the guy with the steaks, right? First date with Susan, and not that long ago, either. Time flies when you're having fun. Shit. But what the fuck is he doing here in all this traffic, maybe he really is out of his mind like everybody else seems to think. But then he looks over at the girl and she's sitting up all perky in her silver ball cap like a little bird or something, looking all around like she's on a tour, smiling at him.

"Oh, Mister Atlas, this is so exciting, isn't it? Miami must be one of the biggest cities in the whole world!"

That's what she says. Exciting.

"Yeah, honey, you got it." He has to grin, passing a semi, what the hell. And then here comes a motorcycle right past the Porsche like a bullet, like a bat out of hell. "That's a young person on that motorcycle," he says. "Young people are the ones on the motorcycles. They don't believe they're ever gonna die."

"Oh, that's not true! What about all those guys with the white ponytails on the motorcycles in Key West? They're all over the place."

Yeah, she's got a point. Smart little thing. He'd have a ponytail, too, if he had any hair.

"'Lion Country Safari!'" She likes to read the signs out loud like she's a tour guide or something. "Ooh that sounds just amazing. I guess we couldn't possibly . . ." She looks over at him.

He shakes his big head, *no*, suddenly remembering the time he took Susan to Africa, yeah now that was a safari all right, that big bull elephant that charged across the road with its ears out. Now that was something. But this girl, it's like she's never been anywhere, anyplace at all. What's with that?

"Oh, look at this one!" She reads it out. " 'Ron Jon Surf Shop. Who Knows Who's Nice?' Now what's that supposed to mean?" She's giggling now, she's having a ball, what the fuck.

"Damned if I know," he says. "Crazy people down here." Which would cover pretty much all of South Florida.

"Pompano Beach! Deerfield Beach!"

So now she's an announcer.

"Boca . . .Boca . . .?" She looks over at him doubtfully.

"Raton," he says. "Like baton, like a majorette has. It's French."

"French for what?" she asks, but then her voice changes

and she says, "Oh, Mister Atlas, oh look, there's a sign for Del Ray Beach, isn't that where . . . ?"

"Yeah." He floors it.

She leans closer to peer at him from beneath the silver brim of her hat. "That must make you so sad," she says. "Don't you want to go over there right now and see Miss Susan? See how she's doing?"

"I'll see Miss Susan soon enough," he says.

"But Mister Atlas—"

"Listen, kid. You wanna go to Orlando, we're going to Orlando. Case closed."

For a minute she looks like she's going to cry, then bites her lip, settling back into her seat for a while like she's pouting. So let her pout. Kids don't know nothing.

"Palm Beach" is her next announcement. Then "West Palm Beach."

"That's where all the rich people live," Herb tells her. Anybody else would already know this.

"Well, they can't *all* be rich," she says. "Somebody has got to cook their meals, fix their hair, do their nails . . . hey, maybe I ought to move there."

"Maybe." He's gotta grin, she's a real character, this little girl.

"Juno Beach." She's reading the names off again as he drives north up Route One. "Jupiter." Then "Port St. Lucie—"

"Hell, that's the Mets!" Herb perks up. "Always been the Mets."

"What? What's that?"

"Spring training camp for the Mets."

"What? What kind of camp?" She cocks her head with the little bird look. "What is the . . . the . . . Mets?"

"Shit, honey. Where'd you grow up, anyhow? On the moon?"

"Sort of." She's laughing again.

So Herb explains the whole thing to her, spring training, getting kind of worked up because it's all changed now, yeah, it's all different, it's ruined, everybody except the Mets has vamoosed. "The Dodgers used to be right back there in Vero Beach, remember Vero Beach? Of course not! So now they're in Arizona, the Red Sox, too—they used to be over in Winter Haven, now they're in fucking Arizona, too. What's Arizona got that Florida hasn't got? I ask you. It's about a hundred and twenty fucking degrees in Arizona all the time now. Global warming, yeah it's all true. Don't get me started. And the Pirates? They're in Bradenton now . . . and the Tigers, the Tigers used to be in Lakelan . . ." Shit! Where are the Tigers now? He can't believe he can't remember.

"Don't get upset, Mister Atlas. I mean, it doesn't matter, does it, where they are now, the—the what? What's the name of them?"

"The TIGERS!" he yells, slamming the wheel so hard he hurts his wrist. "The goddamn Tigers. And hell yes, honey, it does matter. It matters a lot. Everything matters." Though Herb himself couldn't say why, exactly. The things of the world need to stay in one place, their own place, where they belong. Like elephants in Africa. Or Susan in her garden, she loved that garden so much, all those yellow butterflies and red flowers and that big old tree, it was her place. Or like him and

Roxana in the old neighborhood back in Buffalo, they owned that neighborhood, hell they owned the whole town! He thinks again of riding the Cyclone at Crystal Beach, she was hugging his neck and screaming and then they both started laughing and couldn't stop and then they were sitting on the beach running that warm sand through their fingers forever. Now Herb passes a red convertible full of crazy young people and then he remembers him and Susan in this very car, this Porsche with the top down, hell they weren't even young but they loved it, *she* loved it so much, just driving all over the island. She always wore her red scarf and yeah he wore his Panama, it was a real Panama, cost him a bundle even in Havana but yeah, him and Susan on a joy ride, that's what she called it, waving and winking all over town. Well the joy rides are sure as hell over now.

"Mister Atlas, your face is getting real red. Why don't we stop and get some drinks and maybe some more gas?"

She's got a way of calming him down, and she's right about the gas. Anyway, Herb's got to pee something awful, so he takes the next exit, Fort Pierce, which has big signs for the Indian River, the Tropicana plant, the dog track, Hobby Lobby, Denny's—yeah, Denny's are everyplace now, and they won't even give a man a drink.

"Can we please—" she starts in. She's always hungry.

"Nope." He pulls into a Sheetz just in time, well almost in time, and heads for the restroom while she pumps the gas proudly, using his Visa card. When did he give her that card? Damned if he can remember doing it, but who cares? Who gives a shit? This an adventure, right? Lion

Country Adventures, here we are. Right in the middle of Lion Country.

She closes the tank and replaces the cap and flounces into the ladies room as she always calls it, he's gotta laugh at that, and then into the station itself and comes back out with a plastic bag filled with snacks—Cheetos, peanuts, potato chips, Hershey bars, what the hell. She pops open a freezing cold ginger ale for him and a Mountain Dew for herself, then starts eating the peanut butter Nabs the minute she's fastened her seat belt.

"Protein," she announces with her mouth full. "I'm eating for two now."

"So I heard," Herb says, pulling the Porsche back out onto the highway. But he leans over and gives her shoulder a little pat.

"Aren't we having fun?" says Not-Renee.

FIFTEEN MINUTES LATER, that's when they see it, high up. A huge flashing electronic sign like a banner, which extends across the entire interstate highway, Route 1 northbound and southbound, all eight lanes.

SILVER ALERT
PORSCHE CARRERA 2001
CANARY YELLOW VKE
CALL #347

She sees it first. "Look! That's us, isn't it? That's our car! That's us!"

"Well, I'll be goddamned!" Herb strikes the wheel so hard that the Porsche veers into the center lane before he can correct it.

"Mister Atlas, what are you doing?" she squeals.

"Sorry honey. I guess the jig is up." For the first time today, Herb feels really, really old.

"What are you talking about? What's the jig?"

"They've got a police alert out for us, for this car. A Silver Alert—that must be like an Amber Alert, what they put out when young girls go missing. If it's up here, on this highway, that means it'll be up on every highway in Florida, trust me."

She still doesn't get it. "Well, why does it say 'Silver Alert,' then? If it's about us?"

"That's me, honey. I'm old. It's my car. That 'Silver' means geezer, geezer on the run. Dr. Big Shot musta turned me in, God damn him."

"But I'm here, too!" she cries out. "Me too! They've got a police alert out for me, too, don't they?"

"Oh yeah. You bet. And I'm sorry, honey, I'm real sorry I got you into all this trouble. I guess I was using some real bad judgment. It's all my fault, I'll tell them that. You won't get in any trouble, I swear." He could kick his own ass for doing this, stupid old fool. What was he thinking?

But when he looks over at the girl again, she's not heartbroken, she's not crying, she doesn't even look upset. Instead she's sitting up straight in her seat, smiling. Literally beaming. Her whole face is lit up like the sun.

"That's *me*," she says in a kind of wonderment. "That's

me they're looking for, too, on every billboard on every highway all across Florida, all over the state. That's what you said. Florida is one of the largest states in the Union."

"Well, yes it is." Herb has to laugh. "You got that right, honey."

Then he watches in astonishment while she opens her purse and carefully puts on her lipstick. Hot pink. She powders her nose before giving him her biggest, pinkest smile.

"Okey dokey," she says. "I guess I'm ready. We'll probably be on TV, don't you think, since we're so famous? And maybe the internet, too?"

"It sounds like you *want* to be arrested," Herb says. "Is that what you want? Probably the smart thing to do would be just go ahead and turn ourselves in, you know. Right now, next exit."

But she looks so disappointed by this idea that suddenly he's inspired, what the hell, he's old, who cares, who gives a shit, who *really* gives a shit? "*Or*," he continues carefully, "if you really wanna make a run for it, we can go on to Orlando, spend the night, see the damn Princesses and then come back and face the music."

"What music?" she asks, thinking maybe she'll get a chance to sing, in front of all those cameras. Maybe she'll be *discovered!*

"That's just something people say, honey. There's not gonna be any music. That I know of," he adds when her face falls. "So where we gonna spend the night? How you gonna meet the Princesses?" He's just humoring her now.

She settles back and fishes around in the big silver purse,

coming up with her cell phone, his credit card, and a Disney brochure.

"Hey, where'd you get that?" He means the credit card, then he remembers that he gave it to her when she pumped the gas.

"Oh, I've had this forever!" She waves the Disney brochure in the air. Paula always said, Never give up your dreams. "I've been keeping it just in case, and now, look! Ta-da! So you will be very glad to know—" she says importantly—"that you do not have to spend a lot of money and get tickets for the whole thing. We can just get some—wait a minute—" She consults the brochure. "'Fast Passes to meet the Princesses at the Town Square Theater on Main Street.' That's the best place. You never know which ones are going to be there, but it's always at least six, a minimum of six Princesses is guaranteed. So you want me to get the Fast Passes?"

"Sure, honey, go ahead and do it." Herb is amazed. He doesn't actually think she *can* do it, that she knows how to do it, but then she *does*, she's talking to somebody and then she's reading the numbers off his silver Visa card very carefully one by one into the phone.

"Expiration date 2025."

Ha! He'll be dead by then, Herb realizes.

"And the security code is six six nine," she continues.

Uh-oh.

"Thank you very much!" Not-Renee is glowing. "Now that's all done. But where will we stay? They've got hotels all over Disneyland but it's really huge and only a few of them are the Downtown Disney Hotels." She starts reeling off the names.

"Wait just a goddamn minute. This has gone far enough, sweetie," Herb says in the voice that means business, the voice he used to fire people.

She seems to shrink in her seat, looking at him. "Mister Atlas?" Suddenly she acts like she doesn't know him. Well, maybe she doesn't know *this* Mr. Atlas, the boss. The old boss.

"Okay," he says. "Okay on the Princesses, you're gonna see the goddamn Princesses. Okay on the one-day pass to see the Princesses. I'm gonna be waiting for you at some motel, and it ain't gonna be any Disney Downtown Resort hotel either, I can tell you that! Look at me, honey! They wouldn't even let us in. If they did, they'd be crazy. Nah, I tell you what, we'll just lay low, someplace cheap on the way into town where they don't care who stays there, and in the morning, you can take a cab over to the park, and then you can take a cab back to the motel, and then we'll get the hell out of Dodge."

What is Dodge? she wonders.

"You following me, baby? Because this is the only way it's gonna happen."

"But you won't get to see the Princesses!"

"Honey, I don't give a shit about the Princesses," he says. "You're the only princess I'm interested in. So you go over there, and you have breakfast with the Princesses, and then you come back, and we'll take off."

Hell, now she's crying.

Swerving the Porsche, Herb sticks his hand out to her and finally she takes it, her soft little hand as small as a child's. Hell, she practically *is* a child! He could probably get life for this! And what'll he do without his medication, thirteen pills a day? Can he sleep? Can he eat? Shit, he might die.

"Okay, honey, you got it?" he asks.

"Oh, Mister Atlas, you're just the best! And yeah, you bet! I got it!" And she's smiling again as she settles back into her seat.

AT FORT PIERCE they take the exit for I-95 and pull into line for the tollbooths stretching across the entrance to this big highway, which will take them the rest of the way to Orlando, 130 miles. Too far, which is something Herb knows and she doesn't know yet. This is not gonna be easy. The Porsche idles in the long lane, which says NO SUN PASS, while the rest of the traffic goes straight through the booths, flashing their Sun Pass cards. So Herb's gotta pay cash, but how much cash? Who knows?

"Get me some money, honey." He flips up the console between the front seats, where his money bag is.

She fishes around in it. "You don't have any change, or hardly any little bills, nothing but twenties," she reports, just as the NO SUN PASS booth opens up and he's gotta step on it.

The woman in the booth is a big redhead who looks like she's been around the block a few times. Actually she looks something like Pat . . . Pat of Pat and Maribeth, back in Key West, worried to death by now, of course . . . what the fuck is he doing?

Not-Renee hands him the twenty and he gives it to the hefty woman in the booth who seems to be taking her own sweet time with the whole deal, smoothing out the bill, making the change—then leaning out her window past him to peer at the girl, who gives her a big pink smile and a little wave and says, "Thank you so much, ma'am. You have a nice evening, now."

Shit. Why'd she have to say anything? That makes them memorable, Herb knows, as if the yellow Porsche and the girl herself aren't memorable enough. Herb can still see the woman in his rearview mirror leaning out of her booth to watch them as he pulls away, onto I-95 now. He speeds up and enters the flow of traffic.

Fly Away

~~~~~~

"Sebastian." I read the sign out for the old man. Then "Palm Bay." Then "Melbourne." These last two, Palm Bay and Melbourne, are real big places I think. You can tell by the signs, they're bigger now, and also there's more traffic. I'm getting real excited! All these years I've been dreaming about the Princesses, I never thought I'd really see them or go there. Never, never in a million years. It was just something me and Tamika talked about, just a friend girl thing, her and me, and now I'd give anything if she was here, too. She'd be having a fit. Her eyes would get all big the way they do.

"Some day my Prince will come, some day my Prince will come," I start singing to calm myself down so I won't cry but then Mister Atlas says, "Can it, honey. For God's sake."

"What? What is that?" I have to ask.

"That means shut up! You're making me nervous, all right?"

"Yes sir," I say, and I try to can it, but now I'm getting

nervous, too, and also my phone keeps vibrating against my leg. Who is trying so hard to call me? Who? Maybe it's Willie who will be so surprised when he finds out where I went, me and my baby without him, serves him right! All of a sudden I'm real mad at Willie. But my phone is so *persistent* (word), it keeps on vibrating, it could be Tamika, too. Or even Miss Pat or Miss Maribeth.

"Uh oh," Mister Atlas says. "Shit." He slows down and I look up to see the SILVER ALERT sign again, stretching across all four lanes of I-95 North.

SILVER ALERT
PORSCHE CARRERA 2001
CANARY YELLOW VKE
CALL #347

So I hold my phone up and take a picture, which turns out to be perfect, just beautiful in the light of the setting sun. "Yay! I got it!" I cry out.

"What? What the fuck do you think you're doing?"

"This is for me," I try to explain. "I will remember this for the rest of my life, and so will my sweet baby, Tropicana."

"Now that's ridiculous." Mister Atlas has this way he sounds like he's growling. "You can't name her for a brand of orange juice. For Christ's sake."

Which gets me giggling, of course, and even old Mister Atlas has to smile, settling back to drive.

"'Cocoa Beach,'" I read out loud, which makes me hungry. I love cocoa, I get the kind in little envelopes with little tiny marshmallows already in it. Then comes a big sign for the SPACE COAST, Exit 205, which looks real important but sounds like TV.

"What's that?" I have to ask him. "The Space Coast, I mean."

"You're kidding me." Mister Atlas looks over at me. "That's the John F. Kennedy Space Center. It's coming right up. That's gonna be our turn. You know about Cape Canaveral, where they launched the first successful space shot and human beings walked on the moon for the first time. Neil Armstrong, that's the first guy that walked on the moon."

"Oh yeah, I did hear something about that," I tell him, which is true.

And I'm going to tell my baby about this for sure, that she was actually *here*, right here where it all happened. The moon shot. By the time she's all grown up, she can probably walk on the moon herself if she wants to. Maybe she'll be the first girl on the moon! Which just tickles me to death to think about but also makes me cry for some reason.

"Blue Moon, I saw you standing alone, without a dream in my heart," I start singing, it's a sweet, upbeat song.

"I told you!" Mister Atlas is almost yelling in his mean voice but I know he is not really mean.

"Okay, I'm sorry," I say.

But my phone keeps on vibrating against my leg so finally I just can't stand it anymore, I get it out and click it on.

But Mister Atlas starts having a fit. "Renee? What's going on, honey?"

"None of your beeswax," I say, which is something funny Mama used to say, but Mister Atlas is not kidding.

All of a sudden he makes a big *lunge* (word) across that middle seat thing and grabs for my phone—he won't ever wear his seat belt—and right then is when we hear the first siren real close behind us as we head up the ramp to a big bridge.

"Renee! You give me that now, honey!"

The siren sound is louder now it is piercing and over-whelming (words) so I turn around to look and what do I see but two police cars with flashing lights closing in on us and one more way back behind them passing everything just like on TV.

Oh gosh, we are really famous now!

"Renee! What's going on here? You hand over that god-damn phone right now!"

But all I can do is hold on to my baby real tight with both arms as our porch car *veers* (word) to the right and Mister Atlas yells "Get down, honey! Get down!" pushing me down and then we hit something real hard and then we go

flying

flying

flying through the air

Coquina

Well I'm finally out of my brace now and taking classes over at the college, and it is so much fun! Though it's a lot harder than Willie said it would be. I have just *now* gotten that GED he said was going to be so easy because guess what, whoever heard of Pearl Harbor? Or filibusters or Martin Luther King or gerrymandering or gerunds? Lord! I didn't know anything. I didn't even know where I was in the world or where I was going when I got on that bus to Florida, I didn't even know Florida was *south!* Lord! I hoist my bookbag up on my shoulder, shut the red door of the small white house carefully behind me, then stop to catch my breath. It's still kind of hard for me to take a deep breath. And it's hard to keep everything organized—the bookbag for class, the diaper bag, all my nail stuff, it's like I've got to be several more people now. I run my hand along the pebbly white wall of the house for luck. This whole house is made of shells, some kind of concrete filled with little round shells, it must be thousands and thousands of shells, I just love it!—fingering the shells right now. My little house looks real sweet like a fairytale house but kind of prehistoric simultaneously, like a dollhouse made by a dinosaur. *Coquina* is the word, these are coquina shells from the bottom of the ocean, and this house is one of a dozen coquina houses built back in history for cigar makers who came over from Cuba to make cigars here in Key West, right up the street in the Gato cigar factory, which is the women's center now, Safe Harbor. They own these little houses, too, and I know I am very lucky to live here, I am very lucky to be alive at all. This is true of every person alive in the world of course but not everybody knows it. I know it though, me Dee Dee! And I am lucky to know it, and I will never forget it, any of it, never not ever, especially Mister Atlas RIP, which means Rest in Peace. I still miss him.

When I get to the road, I turn back to wave to Atty as Maria holds him up to the window. Atty loves to touch the coquina shells, too, he tries to pull them out of the wall and sometimes he gets one loose and plays with it, which is okay now since he's quit putting everything in his mouth like he used to. Atty—that is Ira Atlas Mullins, what a big name for a little boy!—is actually getting to be a big boy now and he is not scared of a thing. He kind of struts along with his tummy stuck out just like Mister Atlas his namesake did except he's always got a big smile on his face, too, which Mister Atlas did not necessarily have. But oh Mister Atlas would have just *loved* him! Everybody does. I would think that Atty came down from Heaven if I believed in Heaven but you know what? Maybe he did. Maybe Mama's up there, too, and my baby sister Ida Rose and Daddy and Ira, dancing on his box. Somehow it's like having this baby has given them all back to me again, my own family that I really did have once upon a time, a long time ago. I had almost forgotten about them.

I wave again and Maria makes Atty wave his fat little arm, too, before she leans over to put him down. Maria is small, and he's getting almost too heavy for her. Maria comes to babysit on class nights. Now Atty is making funny faces, why he is just a goofball! Atty was an easy baby and he's going to be an easy big boy, too, you can just tell. He is always smiling and running forward real fast.

Atty goes to daycare at the center with me, which has worked out real good. Part of the court deal was that I had to accept counseling over there, but now I work there, too. I started out in daycare but now I'm also teaching manicure and pedicure skills in the self-esteem program and helping with the story circles and actually leading the singing group Free Bird every afternoon outside on the back patio, when the weather is good, or in the Great Room if it's not. Also, I made up the name Free Bird, I am real proud of that! It just came to me one day out of the blue and I told everybody and they all loved it! Now Free Bird sings all over Key West for festivals and the Farmers Market every Saturday morning and even a New Orleans funeral march one time, right down the middle of Duval Street. And some of these women can really *sing*, too! Like the Cuban girls Luisa and Angelina, though there's nobody in Free Bird that can sing as good as Tamika or ever will be, I know that. Tamika has got a place in Free Bird and a bed at the coquina house forever if she wants it, if she ever comes back. I'm still looking for her just like Anna in *Frozen* was always looking for her sister Elsa, Tamika is my sister frozen in ice. I've got an extra twin-size mattress down on the floor in the bedroom just waiting for her, of course Atty plays on it all the time now and that's all right. They will have the biggest time together, and Tamika will be so surprised to meet Atty!

Also Tamika could sing at the Little Room with Ricky when he's in town. But Ricky swears he doesn't know anything about Tamika or Tony, either one. He just shakes his head and spreads his arms out. Now I'm more worried about Tamika being able to find us when she comes back because that little trailer park is going to be demolished any day, a big new hotel named the Ambassador is going in there. Everybody has already moved out of the trailers and campers, which are just sitting there empty and sad, like old toys at the dump.

I always take one last look back at the coquina house before I turn the corner. I always think it's going to disappear while I'm gone. But Lord! The bus is already here so I've got to swing up fast, which is not easy, but then I get a whole seat to myself. So I can settle down and take out the blue notebook to look at what I wrote down last time for English 100, Mr. Ronald Richardson-Gray. I have never heard of a man with such a name as that! He's a tall, bent-over man with wire-rimmed glasses that make his eyes look real big and a kind face and a plaid cap with pieces of long gray hair coming out from under it all around. He looks like he ought to be on one of those Masterpiece Theater shows. But he doesn't sound like that. He sounds nice, tired. Mr. Richardson-Gray said that this class will have a theme, it is *The American Dream*. We are all going to read some short stories and then a famous book named *The Great Gatsby*, which I haven't got yet, I'm thinking I will try the library at the center before I buy it. In addition to Basic Skills such as sentences and paragraphs and outlining and how to write essays, Mr. Richardson-Gray told us that we will need a whole new vocabulary for discussing literature and then he began writing words up on the blackboard.

I still can't decide if Mr. Richardson-Gray was coming on to me or just being nice, but he stopped me after class last week and said to let him know if I need extra help since this will be my first class on the college level, well fuck him! But maybe not. Not everybody is a *villain*. I have got to remember that. *Villain* is one of the new words, which he wrote on the board. Maybe Mr. Richardson-Gray is just nice. He might even be gay, he's so nice. I look at the other words in my blue notebook. They are Plot, Setting, Theme, Conflict, Hero, Anti-hero, Symbol, Setting, and Protagonist. The protagonist is the main character. These are some of the words we will use in talking about stories, about literature, Mr. Richardson-Gray said. Then he explained what these words mean.

As the bus goes through the big stone gates onto the campus, I read over what I wrote down in the blue notebook. This stuff about stories is real different from sitting in the story circle with Mrs. Dellinger and the other girls when I first started coming to Safe Harbor and we all had to tell our stories, and I had to tell what happened to me, that's when I found out that I was a victim of sex trafficking, words I didn't even know. Now, I am leading these story groups myself. And suddenly I've got an idea. From now on, whenever I lead the story circle, I am going to change it. I'm not going to say the word *victim*. I am going to say, This is a story about sex trafficking, and I am the *Protagonist*. Me, Dee Dee!

ACKNOWLEDGMENTS

With deepest thanks to

Mona Sinquefield
Jill McCorkle
Liz Darhansoff
Frances Mayes
Ippy Patterson
Cathy DeSilvey
Alice Gorman

In a lifetime of writing I have been fortunate to have wonderful teachers and editors along the way, starting with my first writing teacher and lifelong mentor, Louis Rubin at Hollins College; peerless editors Faith Sale and Shannon Ravenel; agent Liz Darhansoff, who has stuck with me through everything, since we were young; my husband, Hal Crowther, wordsmith with a perfect ear; and now my wonderful editor Kathy Pories at Algonquin, the very best ever! As Silas House once said, "She's slow as molasses, but she'll dog you to death till you get it right!" She will, too. And so will the indefatigable Chris Stamey. Thanks and love go out to my children Page Seay and Amity Crowther and her husband Michael Ferguson; and to my grandchildren, Lucy and Spencer Seay of Nashville and Baker and Ellery Ferguson of Raleigh. I am so grateful.

"All the Pretty Horses" is an old folk song, quoted here as sung by Jean Ritchie, Kentucky balladeer.

Silver Alert

Questions for Discussion

QUESTIONS FOR DISCUSSION

1. What do you think attracted Herb and Susan Atlas to Key West? If you have been to Key West, what is it about this place that appeals to people?

2. Herb has choice words for a number of people, or if he doesn't say them out loud, choice thoughts. What do you think Herb is so angry about?

3. What does Dee Dee give Susan that her children and husband can't?

4. How do you feel about the children's decision to intervene and place Herb and Susan into a retirement home?

5. Have you or a relative ever been urged into a retirement home? In what ways did they, or you, face issues similar to Herb's? How would it feel to have one's children make this decision?

6. Why does Dee Dee feel the need to lie about who she is? How would she have been treated by the Atlas family and Willie if they had known her true identity and history?

7. Why does Dee Dee keep repeating "word" and trying to expand her vocabulary? What kinds of power can words give us?

8. What is it that Herb gets from Dee Dee? And what does Dee Dee get from Herb? What makes their relationship work? Do you think it's due to the age difference? Would they have been such good companions if they were closer in age?

9. What do you think Herb learns from his ride with Dee Dee up the Keys?

10. In what ways are Herb and Dee Dee similar?

11. How did you feel about Willie? What do you think he saw in Dee Dee? To what extent did his idea of Dee Dee depend upon her being less educated and less worldly?

12. In what ways is this novel about class distinctions? What do Herb and Willie get to do as a result of their social class?

13. What is the significance of the final lines of the book where Dee Dee names herself as the Protagonist?

14. The structure of *Silver Alert* is different from Lee Smith's earlier work and that of other novels; Lee says she saw each chapter as a separate scene with its own title, like a painting on the wall in Susan's art gallery. She envisioned her readers as the visitors to the gallery, passing through, moving from

section to section, scene to scene. In a way, this structure honors Susan, who is no longer her former self but who is absolutely central to this story. How did you feel about the structure of this novel? Did you enjoy visiting these different scenes and places, or did you find it confusing?

15. The journey is one of the oldest plots in literature—starting way back with legends and folktales and *The Canterbury Tales*. The plot of a journey is so effective and satisfying because it comes with a beginning, middle, and end. What other books involving a journey have you read?

LEE SMITH is the author of fourteen novels, including the *New York Times* bestseller *Fair and Tender Ladies, Oral History, Saving Grace,* and *Guests on Earth,* as well as four collections of short stories, including *Me and My Baby View the Eclipse* and *News of the Spirit.* Her novel *The Last Girls* was a *New York Times* bestseller as well as a co-winner of the Southern Book Critics Circle Award. A retired professor of English at North Carolina State University, she has received an Academy Award in Literature from the American Academy of Arts and Letters, the North Carolina Award for Literature, and the Weatherford Award for Appalachian fiction.